CW01670323

SHRINE TO MURDER

An enthralling crime mystery full of twists

ROGER SILVERWOOD

Yorkshire Murder Mysteries Book 15

JOFFE BOOKS

Revised edition 2020
Joffe Books, London
www.joffebooks.com

First published in Great Britain as
***Shrine to Murder* 2010**

ISBN 978-1-78931-427-4

CHAPTER ONE

14 CREESFORTH ROAD, BROMERSLEY, SOUTH YORKSHIRE, UK 0200 HOURS SUNDAY, 24 MAY 2009

The sky was as black as fingerprint ink.

A man in white placed a ladder under the window of a bedroom on the first floor of the detached house. He looked round then climbed rapidly up it. A few moments later he opened the window to its fullest extent and climbed inside.

The only sound to be heard was the heavy, even breathing from a big man in a large bed. The intruder could just make out the outline of the sleeping figure, on his back with his head on the pillow and covered with blankets up to his chest.

The man approached the bedside.

Suddenly the sleeping man's eyes clicked open.

The intruder saw the man's eyes reflect what little light there was. He rushed forward and put a hand across the man's mouth.

'Quiet,' he snapped. 'Not a sound, Redman.'

The man in the bed saw the glint of a shiny dagger blade in the intruder's other hand. His eyes shone like a frightened cat in headlights. His pupils travelled from right to left and then back again.

'Listen to me, Redman,' the man in white said. 'You've done very well for yourself these past twenty years. Made yourself a nice little packet. This place here and your villa in Spain. Two sons both doing well. Both married. Given you three healthy grandchildren.'

Redman's arms came out of the bedclothes and grabbed hold of the intruder's wrist.

'No you don't. *It's payback time, now,*' the intruder said, then he brought the dagger down and stabbed Redman in the chest.

The old man cried out. His heart exploded. Hot blood spurted out over his neck and chest. His eyes centred on the ceiling and stayed there for two seconds; then his eyes closed and his limbs loosened for the last time.

The intruder looked down at the bed, his eyes glowing like cinders. A volcano raged in his chest. His breathing was noisy, his head as light as a champagne bubble. He stared down at the body and smiled. After a few moments, he withdrew the dagger and wiped it on the bedclothes.

*

DI ANGEL'S OFFICE, BROMERSLEY POLICE STATION, SOUTH YORKSHIRE, UK 0830 HOURS TUESDAY, 26 MAY, 2009

'Come in,' Angel called.

It was Police Constable Ahmed Ahaz.

'Any signs of that new sergeant?'

'No, sir,' Ahmed said.

Angel sniffed.

A new sergeant was due. The appointment had been made to replace the irreplaceable Ron Gawber, the much missed man who had been Angel's sergeant for ten years and had recently left Bromersley force for a position in Lyme Bay. The move had come about because his wife wanted to be near her father since her mother had died of cancer just before the previous Christmas. Their two sons had both left home to attend further education. There was a vacancy in the local police force down there so Ron Gawber applied for the post and had got it.

Angel wasn't at all pleased, but he knew Gawber's wife was as masterful as his own wife, Mary. But in his case, he was absolutely certain in his own mind that he wouldn't move away from Bromersley until he was retiring age, whatever scheme Mary concocted.

Anyway, Ron Gawber's replacement was due that morning.

'His name is Carter,' Angel said. 'Show him in as soon as he arrives.'

'Right, sir,' Ahmed said and went out.

Angel reached for the mornings post still untouched on his desk.

The phone rang.

He looked at it and frowned then snatched it up. It was a young constable on reception. 'There's DS Carter arrived here, sir. Asking for you.'

Angel looked at his watch. 'About time. Have somebody show the new DS to my office, lad. And make it quick.'

'Yes, sir. Right, sir.'

He replaced the phone.

He stood up, turned round and looked in the mirror. He adjusted his tie. Then ran a hand over his hair. It wasn't necessary, but he wanted to look his best. He expected his plainclothes staff always to look smart even though they were not in a formal uniform. There were no jeans and T-shirts with slogans (unless the staff were under cover and it was absolutely necessary) on his team. After all, first impressions and all that. He wanted the new man to understand that he was joining a smart, hard-working, no-nonsense, tightly run investigative team dedicated to fighting crime and committed especially to solving murder cases. He had already missed the presence of Ron Gawber. Carter was going to have one hell of a job to come up to his standard of police work, comradeship and perhaps, most of all, dependability.

There was a knock at the door.

Angel turned to face the door.

'Come in.'

The door opened, a uniformed constable put his nose in and said, 'DS Carter, sir.'

'Thank you, lad,' Angel said.

'There you are, Sarge,' the constable said. Then he pushed open the office door and dashed off up the corridor.

As the door swung open, it revealed a pretty brunette in a dark suit and white blouse.

'DS Carter reporting for duty, sir,' she said sweetly with a smile.

Angel's jaw dropped. His face went as white as the padre's knees.

After a moment, Carter said, 'May I come in, sir?'

Angel blinked and said, 'Yes.'

She closed the door and went up to his desk.

'I'm afraid there must be some mistake,' he said.

'Oh?' she said, eyebrows raised.

He screwed up his eyes. 'Well, you're a woman,' he said.

'You noticed, sir,' she said with a smile.

Angel wasn't in any joking mood. His face was as hard as Dartmoor stone. 'I was expecting a Detective Sergeant Carter.'

'I *am* Detective Sergeant Carter, sir,' she said.

He shook his head and blew out a noisy breath.

She lifted her head and said: 'Thirty-four per cent of all police personnel are women, sir. But I am sure you know that.'

His eyes opened wide briefly, then he said: 'Aye? Oh yes? Maybe, but I manage a team who catch the worst kind of criminals, sergeant: homicidal maniacs, murderers, rapists, drug runners and the very worst kind of bully boys. I need *one hundred* per cent of my team to be strong enough and dedicated enough to get in there and tough it out, no holds barred, whenever there's need. Don't you see that, missy?' then he added heavily, 'I can't do with a *thirty-four* per cent margin.'

Her eyes flashed. 'I can pull my weight in any situation, sir. And I would point out that my rank is detective sergeant. I prefer to be addressed as sergeant. Never *missy*. If you don't mind, *sir*!'

Angel's face went scarlet.

'Wait here, Sergeant,' he growled.

He crossed the office, went through the door, charged up the green-painted corridor to the top to a door marked: 'Detective Superintendent Harker.'

He knocked on it sharply.

'Come in,' a voice called out. It was followed by a long and loud cough.

Angel opened the door and was immediately engulfed in a cloud of menthol.

A bald man with a head the shape of a turnip and with thick ginger eyebrows was seated behind a desk, which was heavily loaded with piles of paper and paper files. He looked up at Angel, sniffed and said, 'What is it? I am up to my eyes, lad. I am trying to finish the first-quarters stats.'

Angel blew out a sigh then said, 'Carter's arrived, sir. Ron Gawber's replacement. It turns out *she's a woman*.'

Harker looked up at him. 'Course she's a woman. Did you think she was a man in a kilt?'

Angel wasn't amused. 'It's not right, sir.'

'Not right? You can't forever dodge having women in your team, you know, Angel. You're not *that* special. She comes with an excellent record.'

'I am short staffed enough, sir. You know I can't send her in against some of the monsters we have to deal with.'

'You might find what she's short in brawn she makes up for in brains.'

'I wanted a fully qualified, experienced, *male* sergeant. A man with resolve on his mind and fire in his belly. A man I could confidently send out to bring...to bring Jack the Ripper in, if necessary.'

'Well that's hard luck, Angel. *I'd* like a couple of male *or* female accountants to sort out these figures for me, but the budget won't stretch to it. You've got a perfectly competent detective sergeant, who happens to wear a different sort of underwear, smells of soap and always leaves the lavatory seat down. Those little idiosyncrasies will in no way affect her effectiveness as a police officer, so buzz off and get on with your work and let me get on with mine. There's nothing I can do about it.'

Angel stared at him hard, but Harker had turned back to his mound of papers.

Angel went out of the office and stormed down the corridor.

'Thank you for nothing,' he muttered.

He clenched his teeth. His jaw muscles contorted his face.

He arrived at his office and slammed the door. He positioned himself behind his desk. He looked at the determined face of DS Carter, rubbed his chin, picked up the phone and tapped in a number. It was soon answered.

'Send WPC Leisha Baverstock into my office straightaway,' he said, then he replaced the phone then looked back across the desk at the young woman and said, 'Well, Sergeant Carter, I appear to be...stuck with you...on a trial basis. You follow an excellent man who was with me for ten years. We'll have to see how you measure up.'

'I am sure I'll never be as good as he was, sir,' she said, 'but I'll do my best.'

Angel's eyes flashed back across the desk to meet hers. There seemed to have been a sting of sarcasm in her reply, but her face gave nothing away. He learned something about her that was unusual. She could hold a look into somebody's eyes at least as long as he could.

'At least he usually was able to be on time,' Angel said.

'Sorry about that, sir. I did a trial run from home yesterday and it only took twenty-two minutes.'

'That was Sunday.'

'This morning, the traffic was horrendous, sir. And there were hold-ups at every traffic light.'

'It's Monday. Leave home earlier.'

There was a knock at the door.

'Come in.'

WPC Leisha Baverstock came in. Up to that point, she had been regarded as the station beauty. There might be a feeling of competition now that another good-looking woman had arrived at the station.

'Ah, WPC Baverstock,' Angel said. 'This is DS Carter. Replacement for Ron Gawber.'

The two women looked at each other and exchanged smiles.

Angel added: 'Show her round the station. Introduce her to Inspector Asquith. Answer any questions. Make her feel...at home.'

It was Carter's turn to give Angel a quizzical look.

He stared back at her in surprise.

The two women went out. His eyes followed Carter's every move. He was still staring at the door after it had closed.

It took him a little time to settle down and accept that he now had a women sergeant on his team and that he would have to get used to it.

It was about an hour later that he had read and approved Friday's reports, and read and shredded two anonymous letters from cranks. He was beginning to investigate the heavy brown envelope from the Home Office entitled *The Proliferation of Graffiti in the Rural Community* which included a letter, a pamphlet of 148 pages justifying its necessity, explaining how a census was to be taken, four blank forms in different colours to be completed, and a prepaid return envelope to 'Art in the Community', Inverstolly University, Aberflamburyloch, Wales. He was wondering what was the quickest, easiest and best way of disposing of the stuff when the phone rang.

He eagerly stuffed the bumph back into the envelope, and reached out for the phone. From the cough, he knew immediately that it was the superintendent.

'There's been a triple nine. Woman reports she found a dead man by the name of Redman. Appears to have been assaulted in his bed. Uniform say it looks like murder. Informant's name is Krill. Address is 14 Creesforth Road.'

Angel's heart began thumping.

'Right, sir,' he said and rang off. Then he quickly tapped in another number.

It was soon answered.

'PC Ahaz. How may I help you?'

'Ahmed, find DS Crisp and DS Carter and tell them I'm on a triple nine, suspected murder at 14 Creesforth Road. Got that?'

When Angel said 'murder', it sent a shiver down Ahmed's spine. He wondered if he really was in the right job. He desperately wanted to be a detective on murder cases like Inspector Angel but he was always so easily unnerved.

'Right, sir,' he stammered.

CHAPTER TWO

Angel had no difficulty finding the house. Blue lights flashed silently from the tops of two high-visibility police Range Rovers, which were parked bumper to bumper in front of Dr Mac's car and SOCO's white van on the drive at the front of the house. A uniformed constable stood wearing out the front doorstep and trying to look as if he was serving some useful purpose.

Angel parked his BMW on Creesforth Road, and noticed the lace curtains in the front bay window of the house next door move almost imperceptibly as he walked through the drive gate and dodged under the DO NOT CROSS - POLICE LINE tape.

The constable threw up a salute. 'Good morning, sir.'

'Good morning.'

DS Donald Taylor, head of SOCO was coming out of the house to the van carrying a white transit case. He was dressed in the white all-over suit, boots and elasticized head covering.

They met on the front door step.

'Ah, Don. What we got?'

Taylor pulled down the linen mask. 'Good morning, sir. Elderly man, dead in bed, covered in blood. Looks like he's been stabbed. Been there a while. Nothing appears to be stolen. Method of access not known. The man, a widower, lived here on his own. We've cleared the drawing room; his daughter, a Mrs Kathleen Krill, is in there. Wife of Cyril Krill, the property developer, who lives in Sheffield. He's coming over. She found him forty minutes ago. That's about it.'

Angel nodded. 'Dr Mac working on the body?'

'Yes.'

Another constable in white overalls came from round the back of the house. He saw Taylor and Angel and called, 'There's a ladder been left between the garage and what looks like the summer house, sir.'

Taylor and Angel followed him round on fancy cobblestones to the side of the house.

There was a three-piece aluminium ladder wedged between the two outbuildings hidden from the road. They glanced at it.

Taylor said, 'Might be some prints.'

'I'll check it,' the PC said.

Taylor nodded towards him and then he and Angel made their way back toward the front door.

Angel frowned, then looked at Taylor. 'Is it possible that access to the house was through an upstairs window?'

'I dunno, sir,' Taylor said. Then he looked upwards and pointed at the big casement window on the front elevation of the house facing the road. 'That's the room where the man's body was found. The daughter said that when she arrived this morning both doors were locked. I've checked the downstairs windows. They were all closed and locked. I haven't got round to checking the upstairs windows yet.'

'If access was made by that ladder, maybe there would be marks where the ladder was placed,' Angel said. 'You carry on, Don. I'll have a quick look round.'

Taylor dashed off into the house.

Angel looked in the flower border below the window, and found two marks the feet of the ladder had made. Also there were some wallflower bulbs thoughtlessly stamped on and uprooted. He peered eagerly down at the soil and pulled a disagreeable face. There was no chance of detecting a footprint.

The sound of a car pulling up on Creesforth Road caused Angel to look round. The driver was DS Carter. She parked her car behind his BMW, got out and came rushing down the drive, her hair and skirt flying.

'Got here as soon as I could, sir,' she said rushing up to him and smiling.

He didn't return the smile.

She was eye-catching, but looking at her, smiling, willing and so unquestionably attractive, irritated him. Her film star figure and face were wasted in the business of being a copper, indeed, could even be a distraction in the harsh business of solving murder cases. He briskly told her the bare facts of the findings and then said, 'Now do the door to door.'

'When did the assault or murder take place, sir?'

His eyes opened wide and he glared across at her. 'I don't know. That's the point of the door to door. I'm hoping someone may have seen a ladder up there. Now get on with it.'

Her mouth dropped open. She breathed in quickly. Her eyes moistened. She turned away and dashed off.

He saw her face before she turned. He shook his head irritably and stamped into the house.

The long hall floor and large staircase were covered with white plastic sheeting. The first door on the left was wide open.

A woman in a summer dress and a lot of make-up was sitting in an easy chair looking at him. She jumped up.

'What's happening?' she said, her bright eyes glaring at him.

Mrs Krill?' Angel said.

'Of course,' she said.

'Please sit down. I am Detective Inspector Angel. I am very sorry that-'

'Yes. Yes. Yes,' she said. 'What's happening? Has my husband arrived?'

Angel frowned. 'Not yet,' he said. 'I have to ask you a few questions. I understand that you found your father's body?'

'Yes,' she said, her lip quivering. 'I should never have left him.'

'Sit down, Mrs Krill. Please.'

She sat down uneasily. He sat down opposite her.

'He should have been properly looked after...full time. He could have come and lived with us.'

'And what was your father's full name?'

'Luke Lancelot Redman,' she said. 'There was plenty of room. But he wouldn't move. So stubborn, you know. He expected me to move in here and look after *him*. But I couldn't leave my husband - he's a property developer and builder, you know. He would never have moved in here. My daughter's at boarding school most of the time. We could have gone back to live in Sheffield at her holiday time, but Cyril wouldn't hear of it. He needed to be near his business. The trouble is that men are so stubborn, Inspector Angel. Neither of them would compromise. Of course, they simply didn't get on. They never had, that's the truth of it. Both self-made men. You know...clash of personalities.'

Angel smiled gently at her. 'What is the name and address of the school where your daughter is a pupil, Mrs Krill?'

'Why do you want that? My daughter has nothing to do with this.'

'I am sure that what you say is absolutely correct, Mrs Krill. But we have to check everything, you know.'

She glared at him before answering. There was a few seconds' pause before she said, 'Rosehill Academy, Weeton on the Water, Gloucestershire.'

'Thank you,' Angel said as he noted it on the back of an envelope he pulled out of his inside pocket. Then he said, 'So your father lived here on his own?'

'Didn't I just say that? Yes, he lived in this massive four-bedroomed house for more than forty years. My mother died three years ago. I thought he would move then. I begged him to move to be near us...so that I could more easily keep an eye on him, but no. At one point, Cyril half agreed to build a bungalow on some land next to our house in Sheffield. So that Dad would have been in an independent unit virtually at the bottom of our garden. That would have been handy. I could have popped in each day. Of course, Dad wouldn't hear of it.'

'What brought you here this morning?'

'Isn't it reasonable that I would want to see my own father, Inspector?'

'Of course it is, I simply wondered if he had called you or something like that?'

'No. He would *never* have called me. He was craftier than that. If he needed a button sewing on, for instance, he would phone me and ask me if I knew a good tailor. Then I'd ask him why and he'd say it didn't matter, but eventually he'd let me wheedle out of him that a button had come off his shirt. Then I'd get in my car in Sheffield and come over here to sew the button on. He knew I wouldn't let him go out looking unkempt.'

'Have you any brothers or sisters, Mrs Krill?'

'There's just me, Inspector.'

'Did he have a housekeeper or a daily or any domestic help?'

'He did have. Several. Well, more than several, but he couldn't keep them. He was too pernickety and too critical. And he was downright rude to them, as well. He thought he was living in the days of Dickens. He was also very house-proud. Even though he was eighty-two, he did the housework himself. Look round. Everything is spotless and in its place. I have a fulltime housekeeper but I swear this house is cleaner and tidier than mine.'

Angel glanced round the room and he had to agree that everything that had a smooth surface glistened and reflected back at him, it was also noticeably tidy and uncluttered. 'Did he have any friends, or worse, any enemies? Have you any idea why anyone would want to kill him?'

'Certainly not. He was Mr Charm himself to everyone except Cyril and me. You never heard a bad word said about him. You have to remember, Inspector, that he lived in this town all his life. He worked at the Northern Bank for forty-three years. He worked his way up from clerk to branch manager and then on to local group manager. He may have upset one or two people in all that time but not sufficient to give them a reason to...to...'

She had seemed to have been in control, but she couldn't quite bring herself to use the word 'murder'.

'There must have been somebody,' Angel said quickly. 'What were his interests?'

Mrs Krill frowned. 'He hadn't any. He was fond of gardening. He enjoyed the house.'

'No hobbies or sports?'

'No. He had plenty of interests in his younger days. Football. Photography. Am-dram. Golf. He was into all sorts of clubs and activities in his younger days, but as he got older he lost interest and then my mother was ill. He spent more time with her and his outside interests were neglected.'

'Did he have any money troubles?'

'Certainly not. He was well off, I understand. He was always talking about his portfolio of shares, which were coming to me...that I had nothing to worry about...and then there's this house.'

'You are the sole beneficiary?'

'Yes.'

There was the sound of a doorbell. Angel glanced towards the door to the hall. He thought it was the front door.

Mrs Krill looked anxious.

'When did you last see your father alive?' he said.

'Friday afternoon. I came to see that he was all right and to tell him that I was going down to Gloucestershire to visit my daughter. You see, my husband was going to be away at the Solar Heating and Power Exhibition in London. So I thought it would be a good opportunity for me to take a break. If I had thought that this was going to happen, of course, I would never have gone.'

A PC peered into the drawing room, looked at Angel and said, 'Excuse me. There's a Mr Krill, sir. Says he's looking for his wife.'

'That's all right, constable. This is Mrs Krill.'

'In here, sir,' the PC said. 'This is the inspector.'

He stood back to allow a man to enter and then he went out.

A man in an expensively sculptured suit saw his wife, went over to her, took hold of her outstretched arms, gave her a quick kiss and said, 'Oh darling. Are you all right?'

She smiled and nodded. He turned to Angel. 'I hope you're going to get this madman, Inspector.'

Angel gave him his best non-committal nod of the head, several times, then said, 'Have you any idea who might have wanted Mr Redman dead, sir?'

'Not the slightest. He was a great man. He'll be sadly missed.'

'Your wife suggested that you and he didn't quite hit it off.'

The Krills exchanged quick glances.

Mrs Krill said, 'I only told Inspector Angel the truth, Cyril.'

Krill pursed his lips then said, 'It's true. He could be very…very difficult.'

Angel was weighing the answer when Krill said, 'Inspector Angel? Your name is Inspector Angel? You must be the famous Inspector Michael Angel. The man with the same reputation as the Mounties, that you always get your man? I've heard that you have never failed to solve a murder case?'

Angel was momentarily stumped for words. His ears and cheeks felt hot. He licked his lips.

'I *am* Inspector Angel, sir,' he said. 'I don't know about that other stuff. I do my job...the best way I know.'

Krill pulled his head backwards, smiled and turned to his wife. 'We've got the top man, Kathleen.'

'To continue, if you don't mind,' Angel said. 'You were away this weekend?'

'Just two nights, yes. I went to the Solar Heating and Power Exhibition in London, but you surely don't suspect me?'

'No, sir,' Angel said. 'But we check on everyone.'

Dr Mac, in his white overalls, put his head through the door. He was a small, white-haired Glaswegian. 'Excuse me. Have you a minute, Michael?'

Angel rose and went over to him.

Mac gestured to him to come out into the hall and then he quietly closed the drawing room door.

'I'm ready to move the body,' Mac said quietly. 'You'd be wanting to see it afore we do?'

Angel nodded.

Mac came up close to his ear and very quietly said, 'And there's an...an interesting feature to the case, Michael.'

Angel blinked. That *was* unusual. Mac was not a sensationalist.

'Right, Mac,' Angel said, nodding. 'I'll follow you upstairs in a moment.'

Mac turned away.

'Would you find me some gloves?'

'Aye, I'll see to it,' Mac said, calling back over his shoulder.

Angel returned to the drawing room, asked the Krills if they would mind waiting a few minutes, came out and mounted the stairs, carefully keeping his hands away from the heavily carved ornate handrail, and his feet on the centre line of the white plastic sheeting.

He could hear the hum of vacuum cleaners still being used in other areas of the house by SOCOs, and hoped they might be accumulating valuable evidence.

'Second door,' Angel heard the doctor call.

'Right, Mac,' he bawled and made his way along the oak-lined landing to a large double bedroom.

He was met at the door by a SOCO who handed him a pair of white plastic gloves. 'You wanted these, sir.'

'Aye. Ta.'

He put them on and made his way, keeping to the white plastic floor covering, to the bed nearest the bay window where Mac was waiting for him.

The body was on the bed, on its back, covered with bedclothes to the waist. All around was the dark-red stain of dried blood: on the bedspread, the pillows, the bedhead.

Angel peered at the head of the corpse. It flopped back unnaturally across a pile of pillows.

He had seen hundreds of corpses but it always gave him a chilling feeling in his stomach at first sight. The feeling soon left him as his mind routinely assumed the business of searching for evidence to put the killer behind bars.

The sparse covering of silver white hair confirmed that the corpse was of an elderly male. The face was a grey-white colour. Eyes closed. The lips a violet shade. The mouth was wide open, showing a row of even teeth.

He looked up at the doctor.

'What you got then, Mac?'

'A single incision into the aorta, Michael, ensured this man died almost instantly. As you will see, there is an inordinate amount of blood. It would have spurted out under pressure. I think he must have been dead two or three days. I expect the murder was committed on Saturday night/Sunday morning. The weapon was a double-edged sword or dagger that had penetrated about five inches. One stab only, but the weapon was savagely moved around in the wound post-mortem.'

Angel frowned. He pursed his lips. The murder was certainly executed callously, and was likely to have been carried out by a particularly chilling creature, who would have had quantities of blood on his person...his hands and wrists, possibly his arms, certainly on his shirt or coat or T-shirt, and maybe even on his shoes.

Angel sighed thoughtfully. If only he had a suspect. He could have raced off for a warrant, and if the suspect had been guilty, he would certainly have found DNA in the form of the deceased's blood somewhere on him or on a garment in his possession. He had been through that exercise many times over recent years. This time, it wasn't to be that easy.

'Any other injuries, Mac?' he asked.

'Bruising round the mouth and throat.'

'No doubt to stop him calling out?'

'Probably.'

'Fingers, fingernails, hands. Did he try to defend himself?'

'No. No signs of any retaliation. The murder could have been over in a few seconds.'

'Hmm. Hmm. You said there was something else...an interesting feature?'

'Aye, I did,' Mac said. He crossed the bedroom floor to a great rosewood dressing table in an alcove at the foot of the other bed. There was a large swivel mirror on the top of it. 'Look at this,' he said, and he slightly changed the angle of the mirror.

Angel watched him. It caught the light. *And* his attention. He saw large crudely daubed letters in red on the glass.

'The message,' Mac said, 'whatever it means, is painted in blood, what I assume to be the victim's blood. It is a direct message from the killer. I think it says "V to go".'

Angel blinked. The back of his hand and arm turned to gooseflesh. He advanced towards the dressing table and read it for himself.

'V to go?' he said. 'Yes, but what does it mean?'

'V to go?' Mac said. 'V must be short for something or somebody? Like Violet, Vera, Victoria, Victor, Valerie, or Virginia? Virginia or somebody to go where?'

'Is it a place?' Angel said. 'To go? What's that mean?'

'Valhalla. A burial place for a great man?'

Angel rubbed his chin. 'Valhalla? I'll ask the daughter. Is there anything else?'

Mac shook his head. 'Not here. Might be when I get him on the slab.'

A man in white appeared in the doorway. It was DS Taylor, head of SOCO. 'Excuse me, sir, there's a couple of people in the drawing room asking for you. I think they want to leave.'

Angel wrinkled his nose. 'All right, Don. I'm just going down.' He pointed at the mirror.

'You seen this?'

'Yes, sir. Can't make any sense of it,' he said, shaking his head. 'V to go. It's spooky.'

Angel wasn't pleased. He knew it was eerie, but he didn't enjoy a policeman saying so. 'Have you any idea what these letters were made with?'

'A smudge of cloth, sir, I should think. It could be achieved by putting a blood-soaked handkerchief, towel or any bit of rag around a finger and making the letters like chalking on a blackboard.'

He nodded. 'Are there discarded garments or towels or anything?'

'No, sir.'

'I suppose he cleaned himself up in the bathroom?'

'Yes, sir. There's a trail of drops of blood, presumably from his hands. But he didn't use a towel. Must have wiped his hands down his own clothes or brought his own towel.'

'Or taken one that was here with him,' Angel said.

Taylor looked as if he hadn't thought of it.

Angel said: 'Have you found anything to swab for DNA?'

'No, sir. And he was too smart to leave any prints on the taps, switches or doorknobs.'

Angel wrinkled his nose. 'We've a murderer who is forensically aware.'

'Looks like it.'

'The worst kind,' Angel said, pulling a face.

'It is looking like he came up by ladder through the window in here, sir, committed the murder, wrote that stuff on the mirror, went along to the bathroom to clean up, then returned and went down the ladder to make his exit.'

'So you've nothing in the way of fingerprints or footprints?'

'No sir.'

Angel's face dropped.

'Anything in the bags?' he said.

'We haven't finished, sir, but very little. The house is spotless.'

'In that case, whatever you have sucked up must be pretty interesting?'

Taylor shrugged. He clearly wasn't certain.

'Bring them to my office, anyway,' Angel said. 'I want to see for myself. And look after that mirror,' he said, pointing to the dressing table. 'I'll want *that* taking to the station. Preserve that at all costs.'

'Oh *yes*, sir.' Taylor said. He had already anticipated that he would want that.

'Where's the bathroom?'

Taylor went out of the bedroom, along the landing and turned right into the room next door. Angel followed.

'There is a trail of blood on the carpet,' Taylor said.

'In both directions?'

'Yes, sir.'

'So we can take it he wasn't familiar with the layout of the house?'

'Looks like it.'

The bathroom was a large room. It had plastic covering on the floor.

'Where is the blood?'

'There's a trail of blood to this sink. He's run both taps. There were traces of pink, as you'd expect. He didn't use the soap.'

Angel turned and looked at the towel rail. There were two towels folded neatly across the heated rails. There was room for several more.

'He didn't use those towels either.'

'I suppose there could have been three towels there, Don?'

'Yes. Or more, sir.'

'I'll see if his daughter knew.' He remembered she was downstairs waiting for him. 'I'll have to go,' he said and made for the door. 'I'll come back.'

Mac, who had been standing patiently by the bathroom door, said, 'All right to move the body now, Michael?'

'Yes, Mac. Thank you.'

Angel went out of the bedroom and down the stairs.

Mr and Mrs Krill were still in the drawing room. They stood up when he went into the room. Kathleen Krill looked very pale. Angel thought that shock was now telling on her.

'Sorry to keep you,' he said. 'Please sit down.' He turned to Mrs Krill. 'I won't keep you much longer today, but... something has cropped up. Is there anybody in the family, or that your father knew, whose name begins with the letter V?'

Mrs Krill thought a moment, then looked at her husband. 'Do we know anybody, Cyril, whose name begins with V?'

He looked vague and shook his head.

They both turned to Angel.

'I'm sorry,' she said. 'Can't think of anybody. Is it important?'

'It might be. It's incorporated in the phrase, "V to go", daubed on the mirror up there. Does *that* mean anything at all to you?'

Mrs Krill gasped. The whites of her eyes grew bigger. The murderer left a...a message on a mirror?' she said.

'I am afraid so, Mrs Krill.'

She shook her head, found a tissue and wiped her nose.

Krill looked at her and his manner suddenly became assertive. He was no longer interested in the questions. He stood up, reached himself up to his full height and said, 'We really need to be on our way. My wife needs to rest.' He took a business card out of his pocket and passed it to Angel. 'My private address and telephone number are on this, if you need to get in touch with us. I will take Kathleen home in my car, and collect hers later.'

'Very well,' Angel said. 'Thank you, sir.'

Krill pushed his wife gently through the door and followed close behind.

Angel turned away, looked down at the business card, read it and then pushed it into his pocket. He wasn't happy with the way things were developing. He rubbed his hand across his mouth thoughtfully.

DS Carter peered through the door.

'Ah, there you are, sir,' she said brightly and bounced into the room like a teenager just out of school.

He looked up and frowned. He wasn't pleased. 'Did anybody see anything, sergeant?' he said sharply.

She realized that she was at variance with the sombreness of the occasion; it took her a second or two to make the correction.

'No, sir,' she said. 'Nobody saw an intruder or a man with a ladder or anything suspicious the last few days.'

Angel grunted. That was the last thing he wanted to hear. 'Without exception, everybody spoke very well of Mr Redman,' Carter said. 'The lady next door, a widow, who is in her seventies, was particularly upset. She lives on her own and they had become quite friendly.'

Angel took in what Carter had said. He explained the writing on the mirror to her and then said, 'Go back to the neighbour and ask her if she knows anybody or anything beginning with "V" or what "V to go," might mean.'

'Right, sir,' she said and dashed off.

He looked at his watch. It was almost eleven o'clock. He reached into his pocket for his mobile and tapped in the CID office number. Ahmed answered.

'I asked you to find DS Crisp for me. He hasn't shown.'

'He must be on his way, sir. I had some difficulty finding him but he should be with you by now.'

'Well he isn't, lad, and I want him here.'

'He was out dealing with a market vendor who had some bed sheets stolen.'

'Chase him up for me. This is a murder inquiry, and the crime scene's getting cold.'

Angel heard the closing of the front door.

'Hold on a minute, Ahmed.'

Angel went out into the hall. His eyes met those of a handsome young man in a smart suit. It was DS Crisp.

Angel glared at him. 'Where the hell have you been?' he said. 'I can never get hold of you when I need you.'

Crisp affected a look of childlike innocence. It was his speciality, but Angel was well aware of it. 'I didn't know we were on a murder shout, sir,' he said. 'I was taken up with a shoplifting case in town.'

Angel was exasperated beyond measure, but with Crisp it was a waste of time. He ran his hand through his hair and said, 'Come in here.'

Crisp followed him into the drawing room and glanced round. 'Very nice, sir. I wouldn't mind living here.'

Angel pointed to a chair and Crisp flopped into it.

Angel's grip on the mobile tightened. 'Are you still there, Ahmed? He's arrived, at long last! There's something I want you to do. There are a couple of people...Cyril Krill and his wife, Kathleen Krill aka Kathleen Redman. Look them up. See if they're known to us and ring me back.'

Angel cancelled the mobile and dropped it into his pocket. He looked at Crisp. 'Did you hear what I said to Ahmed, lad?'

'A couple of suspects, sir. Husband and wife. Cyril and Kathleen Krill aka Kathleen Redman.'

'They're not exactly suspects. Up to now, they're witnesses. We haven't any suspects.'

'So we're scratching about, sir?'

'That's exactly it, so I want you to find out what you can about her, Kathleen Krill. She's the daughter of the dead man. She went to see her daughter at Rosehill Academy, Weeton on the Water, Gloucestershire, this last weekend. Find out when she went and when she came back. Also find out what you can about her marriage to Cyril. He's a builder and property developer in Sheffield.'

'Right, sir. And do you want me to check out the husband, while I'm about it?'

'No. I'm getting Carter to do that.'

Crisp's eyebrows went up. 'Oh, DS Carter's arrived then? What's he like?'

Angel wrinkled his nose. 'Different,' he said. 'Now push off lad and crack on with it.'

CHAPTER THREE

There was a knock on the door. 'Come in,' Angel said. He looked up from his desk.

It was Ahmed. 'You're back, sir? Those people you wanted me to look up on the NPC...Cyril Krill and Kathleen Krill aka Kathleen Redman are not known to us.'

He didn't really think that they would be, but when suspects are sparse...

'Thank you, lad.'

The phone rang. It was Dr Mac.

'Ah, Michael. I've found two specimen hairs on the back of Luke Redman's hand that are not his.'

Angel's eyebrows shot up. That was terrific news. He pursed his lips as if he was going to whistle, then blew out air without making a sound. He needed news like that to give him encouragement. It was better than a public commendation from old Judge Heneberry.

'Great stuff, Mac.'

'I can only surmise that they came off the murderer's hand or wrist in the course of the assault. The victim was in good fettle even though he was eighty-two. He still had some muscle tone.'

Angel knew it would be a few days before DNA could be determined and the result checked against the national database.

'That's the only lead we have so far,' Angel said. 'Anything else?'

'Nothing that would get you excited, Michael. If there is, I'll let you know.'

He replaced the phone and looked up at Ahmed. 'We might get some DNA off the murderer. Things are looking up.'

'That *is* good news, sir,' Ahmed said.

'Aye,' he said rising to his feet. 'I'm going out. If anybody wants me, I'll be at the Northern Bank.'

'Right, sir.'

*

'I'm Henry Blamires,' the manager said. 'Sorry to keep you waiting, Inspector. It would have been better if you had made an appointment.'

'I certainly would have, if I had had prior information that an ex-manager of this branch of the Northern Bank, Mr Luke Lancelot Redman, was to be murdered.'

'Oh dear,' Blamires said. 'Oh no? I see. I had no idea. Poor old Mr Redman, murdered?'

Angel nodded. 'And I need to speak to everyone who knew him.'

'Yes. Of course. Old Redman murdered. Have you got the man who did it?'

'We're working on it.'

'Oh how dreadful. Now let me see. I remember him, of course. I joined the bank when he was manager, in the glorious days when bank managers were gods. I was also here when he retired. Can't remember exactly when it was. Do you happen to know the date, Inspector?'

Angel frowned. 'No,' he said. 'I have no idea. Would have been a little while back; after all, he was eighty-two.'

'Ah well, he's the sort of chap who wouldn't have retired until he had to, so I expect he retired when he was sixty, so that would be...1987. Good gracious. That seems a long time ago. There weren't many of the present staff here in 1987, Inspector.' He reached out for the phone and tapped in a number. 'Hello, John. I have Inspector Angel from Bromersley police. Do you remember Mr Redman who used to be manager here? No? Oh. Well, anyway, he's been murdered and the inspector wants to speak to everyone who knew him...Yes, murdered...I know. What about John Johnson? Well ask him...No? Right. Is there anybody else? Let me see, they would need to be over forty-one. No? Right. Thank you.'

He replaced the phone. 'There's only me, Inspector. Staff do move around quite a lot these days, you know. There might be somebody who has worked with him, who is now at another branch, Sheffield, or Barnsley or Rotherham or further afield, who might remember him.'

'Thank you, Mr Blamires,' Angel said. 'I'll bear that in mind. Primarily I need to know what sort of man Mr Redman was. What do you remember about him?'

'Well, I was very much a junior when I joined in 1978. I had to report to Mr Redman who gave me a pep talk and was very strict and rather pompous. But as time rolled on, as he got to know you, and if you did your work carefully and properly, he became quite tolerable.'

'Did you like him?'

'Not really. He was all right. As I said, he was pompous, but fair. He never had to ball me out, of course. I was a good employee. Always kept the rules. There are a lot of rules in a bank, Inspector.'

Angel sighed. He knew all about rules. He wondered if Blamires knew about 'Judges' Rules' that are so biased against the judiciary. There wasn't the time to go into that.

'Was he generally popular?' Angel said.

'I don't suppose so, no.'

'Do you know of any member of staff who might have taken a serious dislike to him?'

‘Just about all of us, I should think, at the time. But, I mean, he had to keep discipline, Mr Angel. Managers are responsible for every coin in the strong room. The local directors in Nottingham know exactly how much there is. Then there’s the necessary requirement of accounting for it accurately. Besides that, each branch is expected to make a handsome profit.’

‘Quite so. But was he *so* unpopular?’

‘In my experience, he was, but it would be ridiculous to suppose any member of staff disliked him enough to want to murder him.’

Angel nodded. ‘What about the clients? There might have been somebody he wouldn’t loan money to, for example. Or somebody on whom he may have foreclosed with possibly dire consequences?’

‘I am sure there were, Inspector, but none of them that I know of who would want to see him dead.’

*

Angel returned to his office and was sitting at his desk thinking over his visit to the Northern Bank. It hadn’t produced a single suspect. According to manager, Blamires, Luke Redman would not have won any popularity contest, but there was nobody he could suggest who might have wanted him dead. Angel reasoned that that was only Blamires’s judgement, and he was wondering how he might economically spread the inquiry further afield to other Northern Bank branches or other banks where employees who had known Redman might still be working. It also seemed to him, in view of the time span of twenty-two years, that the likelihood of finding an employee who had worked with Redman and was able to supply any useful topical information about him was fairly remote. He had to consider the cost of manpower and the odds of achieving a positive result. He was still mulling over the question when there was a knock at the door. It was DC Scrivens.

‘Come in, lad. Sit down.’

When Scrivens was settled, Angel said, 'I want you to get some background on a man called Redman.'

He brought him up to date with the murder and the fact that there were no suspects. He told him about the meeting with Blamires and said, 'I want you to contact all the local branches of the Northern Bank, and any other banks around South and West Yorkshire, and see if you can locate anybody who had known Redman and had a motive strong enough to want to murder him. All right?'

*

'Good morning, sir,' Taylor said. He was carrying a bundle of plastic bags and a yellow folder file.

'Come in, Don. Close the door. Have you brought all of it?'

'All that the cleaners sucked up, sir,' he said. 'Every room separately marked. And the photographs.'

'Put the bags on here,' Angel said pointing to the top of the desk.

Taylor lifted up seven transparent bags, each containing small amounts of grey fluff and dust.

Angel raised his eyebrows.

'I said there wasn't much,' Taylor said.

'Have you separated anything out?'

'Nominal amounts, to see if there was anything unusual.'

'And was there?'

'No, sir. It is all carpet fibre, human dust and common earth fibre typically found in domestic premises. Plus a solitary green leaf, presumably blown in through an open door or window or brought in accidentally by an animal or a human on clothing.'

'Let me see that,' Angel said.

Taylor sorted out the bag and pressed the plastic bag hard against the leaf inside.

Angel peered at it. 'It's an evergreen. Mottled. It's a laurel leaf, Don.'

'Yes, sir.' He showed him the label on the bag. 'It's from the master bedroom.'

'The room where Redman was murdered,' Angel said.

'Probably blown in through the open window, while the murderer was climbing in.'

'Do you have a photograph of it in situ?'

'Yes, sir. It was on the carpet at the side of the bed.'

Taylor raced through the yellow folder. He soon found out a photograph of the lone, innocuous laurel leaf on the pink bedroom carpet. The SOCO photographer had sensibly included the side of the bed and a bedside table leg to show the exact place where it had been found. It was about eight inches from each piece of furniture.

Angel studied the photograph for a few moments then said, 'It's an evergreen, Don. It'll stay this colour for some time.'

'I suppose so, sir,' Taylor said. He frowned. 'Do you think it's really significant? It's only a laurel leaf. There are millions of them in the park.'

'I don't know. It's a slightly unusual discovery...in such a remarkably clean and uncluttered house.'

Taylor nodded.

'We need to know if there's a laurel bush in Redman's garden,' Angel said, 'or, if not, are any in the gardens nearby? Also I wonder if it was windy that way on Sunday night. Let's consider if it is plausible that such a leaf could have been blown into the victim's bedroom by mother nature? Right?'

'Oh yes, sir.'

'If it isn't, then we have to assume that it had been brought there by the murderer on his shoes, or in his clothing, or in something else he brought with him or...or in some other way? Anyway I'll be down there soon, I'll have a look round.'

Taylor considered it a waste of time, but that's what Angel wanted and he was the boss. Taylor had learned that he should never underestimate Detective Inspector Michael Angel. His reputation for catching murderers had spread across the UK and beyond. The newspapers wrote him up as if he was a Canadian Mountie: Inspector Angel, the copper who always got his man.

'Right, sir,' Taylor said and he went out.

Angel took a weathered envelope out of his inside pocket and ran down his notes. He spotted something then felt in his side pocket for a business card...Krill's business card. He turned it over and found the home address and the phone number that Krill had written there for him. He reached out for the phone and tapped in the number. It was soon answered by Mrs Krill.

'It's Inspector Angel. Sorry to bother you. Just a little query. I wondered if you knew how many towels there would have been on the heated towel rail in your father's bathroom, that's all.'

There was a moment's silence.

Angel added: 'We are trying to establish whether the murderer took a towel from the rail away with him or not.'

'Sorry, Inspector, I really don't know.'

Angel licked his top lip with the tip of his tongue. 'I wondered...your father was probably a creature of habit...if he had some number that exactly satisfied his...requirements?'

'I really don't know,' she said. 'I'm really sorry.'

'That's all right, Mrs Krill. It is just a detail.'

There was the shortest of pauses.

'Can you tell me, Inspector,' Mrs Krill said, 'when I may be able to...to organize my father's funeral?'

'I'm afraid that there is an inevitable delay. I'm sorry about that. It will be a week or two depending on the progress of the case. I will let you know.'

'Thank you,' she said.

'Have you had any further thoughts about the message on the mirror, Mrs Krill? Does "V to go" mean anything to you at all?'

'I'm afraid not.'

Angel pulled a face. There was no joy there. 'All right, Mrs Krill. Sorry to have bothered you.'

He replaced the phone and immediately left the office for the car park.

He drove the BMW to Redman's house. The SOCOs van and DS Taylor's car were parked outside. The PC was still on the step.

Angel pursed his lips as he ambled round Redman's small front garden. There were no laurel bushes. He went round to the rear of the house. There were two lawns and a small orchard at the bottom, but there were no laurel bushes there either. He returned to the front of the house, went out of the front gate and along Creesforth Road, passing two houses. He peered into their front gardens, stopped, turned round and walked back to the house and looked at the gardens of the two houses at the other side. There were no laurel bushes. It was becoming apparent that the laurel leaf could not have dropped on to the victim's carpet at his bedside without human involvement.

Angel dashed inside and called up the stairs, 'Don Taylor there?'

'Here, sir,' Taylor replied. His head appeared over the banisters.

'Don, is any part of the house still under crime scene protocol?'

'No, sir,' Taylor said as he descended the stairs.

Angel wasn't pleased. 'And you've nothing more for me?'

'Sorry, sir.'

Angel blew out a length of air. He was searching for a forensically aware murderer, and he didn't like it.

Taylor knew he was disappointed. He would have liked to have said something supportive to him, but he couldn't think of anything appropriate at that time.

Angel stood there, looking round and rubbing his chin.

Taylor said, 'Can I help you with anything, sir?'

'Yes. Photographs, Don. Home snaps. You know the sort of thing. Sometimes helps you to build the picture of the victim.'

'Photographs? There are stacks on the walls of that room up there, sir,' he said and pointed along the hall to a room at the end. 'It's a sort of study.'

'Oh, right, Don. Thank you,' he said as he walked down the hall.

Taylor returned upstairs.

Angel found the room had a big desk in it, a filing cabinet, a couple of chairs, a set of golf clubs, and a TV set with a big screen. The walls were covered with a hundred or more framed photographs of the victim, Redman, in every conceivable role: as husband, father, bank manager, president of the Rotary Club, chairman of the golf club, the cricket team, on holiday in Santiago, St Petersburg, Lucerne, Paris, and so on. There were formal photographs of him taking part in local stage productions of *The Gondoliers*, *Nero*, *The Importance of Being Ernest*, *Charley's Aunt*, *Ladies In Retirement*, *Aladdin* and lots more. He was there, singing *The Messiah* with the local choral society at Christmas, enjoying a boat trip on the *Flamborian* sailing out of Bridlington harbour in the summer, and simply peering at unusual objects being petrified in Mother Shipton's cave in Knaresborough in the autumn. The photographs seemed endless. Some showed him alone and some with one or two others and in large groups of thirty or more. Each picture was carefully, neatly captioned in meticulous detail giving names, dates, places and occasions.

Angel was marvelling at the busy life Luke Redman had led when his thoughts were disturbed by the ring of his mobile phone. He dived into his pocket for it. The LCD showed him it was Superintendent Harker. An encounter with his boss was never pleasant, and in anticipation of an unpleasant encounter, Angel's face assumed the appearance of a man with toothache waiting to see the man from the Inland Revenue.

'I've just had a triple nine call,' Harker said. 'A dead woman found in the back room of her florist's shop at 221 Bradford Road.'

It could hardly be more serious. Angel's heart began to thump.

'Name given as Ingrid Underwood,' Harker said. 'Appears to have been stabbed in the chest. Same place as in that Redman case.'

Angel's innards turned a somersault.

'Uniform are in attendance,' Harker said. 'I have advised Mac. Can't raise SOCO.'

'Right, sir,' Angel said. 'SOCO are with me. I'll direct them.'

He pocketed the mobile and made for the hallway. In his head, he heard Harker's voice again say the words: 'Appears to have been stabbed in the chest. Same place as in that Redman case.'

He called up the stairwell to Taylor, gave him the news and the name and address of the shop where the dead body had been reported found, then dashed outside to his car.

He was at the premises in four minutes.

The florist's shop was a very small, commercially well positioned property on the corner of the main Bradford Road and a blocked-off side road called New Street.

Angel pulled past the shop, round the corner, parked behind Dr Mac's car and two marked police cars on New Street.

Two PCs were already rolling out the blue and white DO NOT CROSS tape. Another, PC Brian Donohue, a car patrolman, was speaking to an elderly woman. Angel went up to the two in conversation.

The PC saw him coming.

'Excuse me, Miss Jubb,' Donohue said and turned to Angel. 'Dr Mac is inside, sir.'

Angel nodded. 'Right, Brian, and who found the body and rang in?'

'This lady, Miss Jubb, sir.' He turned back to her and said, 'This is Inspector Angel, he's in charge of the case.'

'Thank you,' Angel said. 'Now then, Miss Jubb, please tell me what happened?'

SOCO's van pulled round the corner on to New Street. Donohue went off to assist with the parking of it. Space was at a premium.

The woman was shaking. Angel took one of her hands. She held it tightly.

'Would you like to sit in my car?' he said. She didn't reply but he quickly led her to it. When they were inside and the doors closed, she was much more at ease.

'I was coming for some flowers,' she said. 'I come here most Wednesdays about this time.'

'Can you say what time that was, Miss Jubb?'

'About twenty to nine it must have been. Well, I went into the shop. The door was wedged open. Mrs Underwood wasn't in the front of the shop. Sometimes she's in the back making up wreaths and displays or whatever. Anyway, I looked at the flowers on display...thinking about what I wanted...while I was waiting. I didn't mind a minute or two, but after I had waited for about five minutes, I called out to her. There was no reply. I waited another couple of minutes then I went into the back, still calling her name. Then I saw her feet and then her legs on the floor in front of the big table she spreads the flowers out on. I thought she had fallen. I went further inside...then I saw the blood...and I knew.'

She paused.

'It *was* Ingrid Underwood?' Angel said.

'Yes. It took me a minute to recover then I looked round for Ronnie, the lad who makes the deliveries. He's usually around. He sits on the step with the shop door open in good weather. He's *always* there. Except that today, he wasn't. That's unusual, I thought. Very unusual.'

'Perhaps he was out delivering?'

'I saw his bicycle's in the back room,' she said. 'He couldn't have been.'

'What's his name?'

'I only know him as Ronnie. Been here years. He's not right in the head, you know. Religious mania. That's what he's got.'

Angel blinked. 'Was Ingrid Underwood married?'

'I don't know, Inspector. I didn't know her well. That lad Ronnie doted on her. It wasn't healthy. Can't imagine what went wrong. Something burst in his head or something. They say the change of the moon affects them, don't they?'

Angel frowned. Her comments disturbed him, but he contained his thoughts. Time was precious. 'Then what happened?'

'Well, then I picked up the phone at the end of the bench in there, dialled 999 and reported it. The woman asked me to wait here, which I have done. I've told you all I know. Now I'd like to go home.'

'Yes, of course. And thank you very much.'

Angel called on PC Donohue to take Miss Jubb home in his patrol car. Meanwhile he rang Ahmed's number on his mobile. As it was ringing out, he watched Taylor and his squad, dressed in fresh white disposable suits begin cautiously to enter the shop.

'Ahmed,' Angel said into the phone, 'I am at a murder scene at 221 Bradford Road. I need Trevor Crisp and that new sergeant, DS Carter, here smartly. Find them for me.'

'Right, sir.'

A man in a khaki overall coat came running up to the DO NOT CROSS tape and attempted to lift it up to gain access. A PC saw him and stopped him.

The man was breathing quickly and his face was red. 'What's happening,' the man said. 'What are all you police doing here?'

'Who are you, sir?' the PC said.

'I own the bicycle shop across the road opposite. My name's Carl Young. Who is in charge? Has something happened to Ingrid?'

Angel came up to him, 'I'm in charge, sir. Do you know Mrs Underwood?'

The man's face was red and his eyes were staring. 'I certainly do. Known her years. What's happened to her?'

'Does she have a husband, and has she any family?'

'She said she was married once. He ran off, I think. I don't know. Got a daughter somewhere. What's happened to Ingrid?'

'There is a report of a body of a woman on the premises.'

'Oh, my god. No. Not Ingrid. Oh no.'

'It may be Mrs Underwood. She has not been formally identified.'

'Oh. This is dreadful.'

'I'm so sorry. We are waiting for the doctor's preliminary report. He's still in there. What was your relationship to her?'

'Just a good friend,' he said with a shrug. 'She's had this shop here for twenty years, the same time as I've had the bike shop over there. We wave to each other, that's all. I keep Ronnie's bike running. I would come over to talk to her when I was slack. She came over to talk to me. She could see if any customers came in here from my shop doorway. We used to see each other open our shops on a morning and lock them up at night. A sort of kinship developed. Oh my god, I hope it's not her.'

'Please try and hang on, Mr Young. Did you see her arrive this morning?'

'Yes. I saw her unlock the shop, and Ronnie began to take the shutters down at about 8.30 as usual. I gave a little wave and she nodded and smiled back.'

'Do you know where she lives?'

'22 Park Road. Have you seen that lad, Ronnie? He's always here. Where's he gone? He's here before the shop opens and he leaves after Ingrid's locked it up. He's always here except when he's delivering or on an errand for her. He should be here. I don't understand it. You know, inspector, he's not quite right in the head. He should be here *now*. He never leaves the shop when she's here, normally. He could have answered all your questions. Typical. The young uns today. When he's wanted, he's not to be found. I reckon he'll know what's happened. Nobody could have harmed her while Ronnie was here. No one could have got near her.

Unless - ' He suddenly broke off. His eyes moved from left to right, right to left and then back to the centre. 'Oh no!' he said. 'Oh no!' Then he looked down at the pavement and shook his head.

'Take it steady, Mr Young,' Angel said. 'Do you know his full name and where he lives?'

'Ronnie Striker,' he muttered. 'He lives with his mother on Church Street. Almost opposite the church gates. I'll have to get back to my shop.'

'Thank you, Mr Young. You've been most helpful.'

He turned away.

A car Angel recognized turned the corner and drove right up to him. It was DS Carter. He bent down to speak to her through the car window. He told her the essentials of the case and set her off to see if she could find Ronnie Striker on Church Street. She turned the car round and dashed off.

The shop door opened and a small man in whites came out. He had a white plastic carrying case hanging from his shoulder. He saw Angel and pulled down his mask.

Angel dashed across to him. 'Mac?'

The pathologist turned up his nose then said, 'Not nice, Michael. Not nice at all. Dead woman, middle aged I should think. Stabbed in the aorta.'

Angel blinked. Mac looked at him knowingly. It was the same injury that killed Luke Redman. 'Is the weapon there?'

'No. And she's not been dead long.'

'Any other wounds?'

'Not that I could see. There is blood everywhere. It's a real mess.'

Angel rubbed his chin. 'Anything to help *me*?'

`Yeah,' Mac said heavily. 'There's another message for you on the mirror in there.'

Angel's heart missed a beat. His fists tightened.

'What's it say, Mac?'

'It says, "IV to go".'

Angel lifted his head. 'Of course, Roman numerals,' he said. 'The "V" in the first message at Redman's was for five.

It's a warning that there are to be four more victims?' He shook his head in disbelief. 'Oh no.'

'Aye, Michael,' Mac said. 'There's no other interpretation that comes to mind.'

The muscles on Angel's face tightened. 'It's a boast...a claim...a statement of intent, from the murderer.'

Mac nodded.

CHAPTER FOUR

Two hours later, at a quarter past two, Angel came out of the grisly flower preparation room, through the shop and outside into the fresh air. He was followed by Taylor, still in his whites.

'I want every bit of greenery on the premises saved,' Angel said, as he peeled the rubber gloves off and handed them to Taylor. 'Doesn't matter how small, how damaged, how lifeless, how insignificant it might be.'

'Right, sir,' Taylor said.

'And that mirror, Ron. I suppose it will unscrew from the wall.'

'Leave it with me, sir.'

'And there'll be Ingrid Underwood's house to go through. The address is 22 Park Road.' He glanced at his watch. 'You'll not get there today.'

'No, sir. Sometime tomorrow morning, I should think.'

'Right, Don, there's nothing more here for the time being,' he said. 'Tell Mac I said it was OK to move the body when he's ready.'

'Right, sir,' Taylor said, and he turned back into the shop.

Angel stood on the pavement and took a few deep breaths. He was glad to be outside and away from scene.

It had been an unpleasant business examining the site. The woman's lifeless white face, the wound, the excessive quantity of blood...and the MO of the murderer of Ingrid Underwood appeared to be significantly the same as that of the murderer of Luke Redman.

He sighed. There was a lot to do and few hands to do it. He pulled out his mobile and tapped in Ahmed's number.

'Ahmed, I told you to get DS Crisp to report at this scene of crime urgently.'

Ahmed blinked several times. 'I couldn't get a reply from him, sir. I tried several times. His phone appeared to be switched off.'

Angel's grip on the mobile tightened. 'It's always switched off. Has DS Carter brought anybody into the station, to interview or anything?'

'No sir. I haven't seen her.'

'Right, lad. I am leaving the flower shop now. If either of them turns up or contacts you, tell them to contact me on my mobile immediately.'

He closed the phone, rammed it in his pocket and got into the BMW. He was angry that he hadn't heard from either of his sergeants. Crisp had always been a bit of a maverick and liable to put himself out of contact for short periods. Angel had told him about it times without number. But he made up for it by almost always coming up with the goods. Angel was surprised at his own patience with the man. However, he was in no mood to allow any slack to the new woman, Carter. If she thought she could sweet talk him with a pretty smile and a whiff of 'Evening in Paris', she had another thing coming.

He turned into Church Street. He was looking for the home of Ronnie Striker. He was pleased to see ahead of him Ron Gawber's car, now Carter's car, parked right opposite the church gates. He pulled up behind it and looked along the terrace of ten houses. He chose the nearest house with the freshly scoured, whitened step and the cleanest front door and knocked on it. It was opened by Carter.

They looked at each other with surprised expressions.

'Oh, sir.'

'What are you up to?' Angel said. 'Why didn't you report in?'

She began to speak, looked behind, then came out on to the pavement and closed the door.

'Never mind,' he said. 'Is the man Ronnie Striker in there?'

'Yes, sir,' she said quietly.

'Has he got an alibi? Did he do it? Why wasn't he at the flower shop?'

'I haven't actually spoken to him, directly,' she said.

'What do you mean? Have you *seen* him?'

'Well, no sir. You see, his mother - '

Angel's patience ran out. 'I told you to interview *him*. Not his mother. I wanted you to *talk* to him. He might hold vital evidence. He *might* be the killer.'

Carter's face went the colour of a judge's robe. 'Oh no, sir. He's not the killer.'

'How do you know?'

'He has learning difficulties, sir. His mother says he has the mental age of a twelve-year-old.'

Angel's eyes flashed. His fists clenched. 'So what?' he said.

He had been about to go into a discourse about children who had committed murder but promptly abandoned it.

'Never mind,' he said. 'Leave it. I'll take over here. Go back to Bradford Road, to the florists. Ask around the shops either side and those on the opposite side of the road. See if they saw any comings and goings, deliveries, customers, anybody, entering or leaving the shop between the time Ingrid Underwood arrived, that was about 8.30, this morning and the time the witness found her dead, that was 8.40.'

'But sir,' she said through clenched teeth.

Angel glared at her. 'Sergeant,' he said.

She hesitated for a second then stamped away to her car.

Angel's face was as long as the list of disbursements on a barrister's bill. He turned round, grabbed the door knob of

Striker's house, turned it, pushed it and banged the knocker at the same time. The door opened and he was inside the little house. He glanced round the room. A plump woman in a rocking chair looked up at him. The chair was at the side of a gas fire set in front of a black stove. She had some knitting on her lap. There were four large coloured prints on the walls of Jesus preaching, Mary and the baby Jesus, Jesus on the cross, and the Last Supper. Also there were figures of Jesus, Mary and the major saints under glass domes on the sideboard. Everything was Victorian, bright, clean and shone like the police parade on November 11.

She looked up as Angel burst into the room.

'Oh,' she said. 'The police lady gone? Who are you?'

'I am Inspector Angel. You will be Mrs Striker? I have to speak to your son, Ronnie, urgently. Is he here?'

'In a manner of speaking he's here, Inspector,' she said.

'Where? I don't see him.'

'He's on the stairs,' she said and pointed with a thumb to a door immediately behind her. 'He's afraid, Inspector.'

Angel heard the door click and saw it open a mere quarter of an inch. He realized that Ronnie Striker was probably peeping at him and would be able to hear every word. He looked away.

'What's he afraid of, Mrs Striker,' Angel said.

'He says he saw Jesus this morning.'

Angel blinked. 'Oh,' he said, rubbing his chin. His mind was trying to make connections faster than a Hewlett Packard.

'And...do *you* think he saw Jesus, Mrs Striker?' he said.

'He must have done. He always tells the truth, Inspector.'

Angel nodded thoughtfully.

'Well that *would* frighten him,' he said. 'It would frighten *me*...but how does he *know* it was Jesus?'

'Well, he said he looked like Jesus. I don't know. But he *knows* his bible. He would *know* whether it was Jesus or no.'

Angel licked his bottom lip then rubbed his mouth and chin very hard.

'That police lady didn't believe me,' she added.

'Well, not everybody understands.'

'She said that something horrible had happened to Ingrid Underwood.'

'Yes,' Angel said. 'We can talk about that later, Mrs Striker. Do you think Ronnie would like a ride in a police car? You could come too, of course. You both could have a look round the police station and I could have a chat with him afterwards, and I'll show him my handcuffs?'

Her face brightened. 'Oooh, I don't know, Inspector. Sounds...very nice.'

The stairs door creaked and opened a few inches.

Mrs Striker heard it. 'That you, Ronnie?'

A big man in a smart suit came into the room. His white hair was plastered down tidily and his skin was grey. He came round the back of the chair into Mrs Striker's vision and stood in front of her. He avoided looking directly at Angel.

'Oh, you've put your best suit on,' she said, smiling. 'You do look smart. Are you feeling better?'

'Yes, Mother,' he said in a voice pitched unusually high.

'That's Inspector Angel, Ronnie. Would you like a ride in a police car?'

He nodded.

Angel came forward, put out his hand, smiled and said, 'How do you do, Ronnie?'

The man looked at Angel, expressionless.

'Shake hands, Ronnie,' Mrs Striker said. 'And thank the inspector.'

The hand felt like a wet haddock.

'Thank you, Inspector,' he said in a forced soprano voice.

Angel nodded and turned away. He really wanted to get on with crucial questions about the murder. He sighed and dug into his pocket for his mobile.

'Can we have the siren on and go at a hundred miles an hour?' Ronnie asked.

Angel looked up, closed his eyes momentarily. Then he turned round, smiled and said, 'Of course you can.' Then with teeth clenched he ran his hand through his hair.

*

Patrolman PC Donohue showed Mrs Striker and Ronnie Striker into Angel's office.

Angel was there with Ahmed, waiting for them.

Ronnie came into the office, his shining eyes looking here and there and everywhere. Mrs Striker followed much more sedately.

'Please sit down,' Angel said. 'Did you have a nice spin, Ronnie?'

His face brightened. 'Yes thank you, Inspector. We did 70 miles an hour and Brian put the siren on,' he said looking across at Donohue.

Angel looked at Donohue.

Donohue nodded to indicate that everything went well.

'Thank you, Brian,' Angel said.

Donohue went out and closed the door.

On the desk was a pair of handcuffs. Ronnie spotted them, and reached out. Mrs Striker saw him and tugged at his jacket sleeve to stop him.

Ronnie frowned, looked across at Angel and said, 'Can I try the handcuffs on, Inspector?'

Angel smiled and said, 'Of course you can, but can you wait until after we've had our little chat, Ronnie? It'll be something to look forward to, won't it?'

Ronnie stuck out his bottom lip and sat down heavily on a chair next to his mother.

'Don't be a nuisance, Ronnie,' Mrs Striker said. 'All good things come to those who wait.'

Ronnie looked at her, wrinkled his nose, shuffled on the chair and began to look at his fingers.

Ahmed pulled out a chair near the door and sat down. Angel looked round and then sat down at his desk.

‘Now then, Ronnie,’ Angel said. ‘I want to ask you a few questions. It’s important that you tell me the truth. You understand what the truth is, don’t you?’

Ronnie didn’t reply. He was more interested in his fingernails.

Mrs Striker jabbed her fingers into his ribs and said, ‘Pay attention to the inspector, Ronnie. Answer him, politely. Come along. Don’t show me up.’

Ronnie looked up at Angel. ‘I don’t tell lies, Inspector.’

‘Good. Good,’ Angel said, rubbing his chin. ‘How long had you worked for Mrs Ingrid Underwood?’

‘I dunno,’ he said. ‘Can’t remember.’

Mrs Striker glared at him and then looked at Angel and said, ‘Since he left the special school, Inspector. That was twelve years ago.’

‘So you know her very well. What time did you start work this morning?’

Ronnie didn’t reply. He looked down at his fingers again.

‘He doesn’t quite know about time, Inspector,’ Mrs Striker said.

The young man looked up. ‘I do,’ Ronnie said. ‘I start at 8.30, but I always get there by 8.20. She makes me go early.’

‘Well, I don’t want you to be late, that’s all,’ she said. ‘It’s the early bird that catches the worm. You should be grateful.’

Angel sniffed. ‘What happened this morning?’

‘The usual,’ Ronnie said. ‘I got there about twenty past eight and sat on the step and waited.’

‘Then what happened?’

‘Ingrid came and opened up, like always, and I put my bike in the back, took the shutters down, put the kettle on like I always do.’

‘Then what happened?’

‘She gave me two pounds and twenty-five pence and sent me out to *The Lunch Box* to get her a sandwich. It’s just round the corner.’

'Does she always do that?'

'Only when she doesn't bring her own.'

Angel pursed his lips. He hadn't heard of the place. 'How long did it take you to fetch the sandwich, Ronnie?'

'I ran there and back, but she had to make them up specially - prawn and tomato.'

'Five minutes? Ten minutes?'

'Ten minutes, I expect. I was as quick as I could run.'

Mrs Striker said, 'It wouldn't be long. He always runs everywhere, don't you Ronnie?'

'Yes,' Ronnie said.

'Yes, I'm sure,' Angel said. 'Then what happened?'

'I went straight through the front shop into the back room,' Ronnie said. 'The shop door was propped open with a brick.'

'Was it usually propped open like that?'

'Yes. In the summer and good weather. I usually prop it open.'

'And what did you see?'

Ronnie's face turned from a grey colour to a sweaty red. His eyes looked straight ahead but he didn't seem to be looking at anything. He didn't speak.

'Yes, Ronnie?' Angel said. 'What happened?'

'Ingrid was on the floor by the table and Jesus was kneeling down in a red cloud praying over her.'

Angel's jaw dropped.

'What did you do?'

'It was amazing.'

'Yes, Ronnie, then what happened?'

'I knew I shouldn't be watching. It was a private moment. He was giving her the last rites so I knew she must be dying. I didn't want to see that. I came out and I ran back home.'

'That's right, Inspector,' Mrs Striker said. 'He arrived home at about nine o'clock. He was in a state, poor lad.'

Angel rubbed his neck and chin. 'What did Jesus look likc, Ronnie.'

He stared at Angel for a moment then smiled knowingly.

'*Everybody* knows what Jesus looks like.'

'Ronnie!' Mrs Striker said. 'Don't be rude. Tell the inspector exactly what you told me.'

'I'm not being rude. Well, he wore...like a long white robe. And sandals.'

'Anything else? Anything on his head?'

'He had long hair.'

'What colour?'

'Brown, I think. It was dark, anyway.'

'Did he have a halo?'

The pupils of Ronnie's eyes slid to the left and then the right. 'I don't know about that,' he said.

'Does that mean no, Ronnie?'

'I can't remember, Inspector.'

'Did he have a beard?'

'I didn't see his face, but I expect so. He would have, wouldn't he?'

'I don't know. I didn't see him. *You* saw him. Are you sure it *was* Jesus, Ronnie? Could it have been a saint or somebody else?'

'No. It was Jesus. He held a star in his hand. It shone so brightly I had to close my eyes.'

'A star?' Angel shook his head. This was getting out of hand. 'What sort of a star?'

Ronnie frowned. 'I don't know. I think he was polishing it on his cloak.'

'What colour was it, Ronnie?'

'I don't know. It was bright. It blinded you. It was wonderful.'

'Was it silver?'

Ronnie nodded.

'And what were you wearing at the time?' Angel said.

'My jeans, T-shirt and trainers.'

'I shall want to borrow those, Ronnie.'

He looked at his mother.

'Yes. Yes. That's all right.' Mrs Striker said. 'The inspector can borrow them.'

Ronnie pulled a face. 'I shall want my trainers, Mother.'

'It won't be for long,' Angel said.

Ronnie looked down at the black polished leather shoes and stamped on the floor several times. 'I can't get round in these shoes. I told you. They're too heavy. I can't run in them.'

'Of course you can,' Mrs Striker said. 'The inspector needs to examine your clothes. Let's have no more argument about it.'

Ronnie wriggled irritably in the chair then went back to looking at his fingers.

Angel licked his lips. He wanted to finish this interview quickly.

'We're nearly done, Ronnie. Just two more questions, then you can have a look at the handcuffs.'

Ronnie looked up.

Angel nodded reassuringly.

Ronnie began to peel bits of loose skin from around his fingernails.

'You said this all happened in a cloud...a *red* cloud?' Angel said.

Ronnie looked up again. His eyes glazed over. Then he said, 'Yes, Inspector. It was all round the Lord everywhere. It was wonderful.'

Angel pursed his lips. 'And what colour red was it?'

Ronnie screwed up his face. 'Just red. Ordinary red.'

Angel said. 'There are lots of reds.'

Ronnie shook his head.

Angel then opened the desk drawer and rummaged around. He found an old stick of sealing-wax. 'That's *one* red,' he said. 'Was the cloud that colour?'

Ronnie put his hand to his chin and rubbed it.

Angel pointed to the tiles on the office floor. 'Those tiles. There's another red.'

Ronnie looked down at the floor, and shook his head.

Deep in the drawer, Angel found a typewriter ribbon he had had for years. It was unused. He hadn't had the heart to throw it away.

'What about that?'

Ronnie looked from one to the other, his lips, nose and forehead twitching uncertainly.

Angel said: 'Just a minute.'

Then he quickly rattled through the morass of pens, pencils and paperclips and other stuff in the drawer and found an unopened packet of white blotting-paper which he opened and put on the desk top. Then he took out a very old razor blade and slammed the drawer shut. The blade was blunt from years of sharpening pencils and other jobs he had found to do with it, and was far from hygienic, but he made a slight cut on the little finger of his left hand, squeezed the finger and applied it to the blotting-paper. A small spot of blood quickly spread to the diameter of a pea. He held the paper up to Ronnie and said, 'Was it *that* red?'

Ronnie nodded. 'Yes, Inspector. *That* was the red.'

CHAPTER FIVE

Ronnie Striker hadn't seemed guilty of any wrong doing, so Angel had sent him and his mother home in a marked car, at least for the time being. He had watched Ronnie jump up and down and clap his hands at the prospect. Angel had also sent a SOCO officer with a sterile bag to collect Ronnie's jeans, T-shirt and trainers for examination.

Angel was still puzzling over the extraordinary evidence Ronnie Striker had given him. He had recorded the interview and played the tape back on the miniature personal recording machine he had concealed under a letter on his desk. It could not be used as evidence, but it saved time trying to remember and write down all the fine points of Ronnie Striker's actual words. It needed some evaluating and understanding.

He rubbed his chin.

There were still a few urgent details to be attended to before he could leave for home. He looked at his watch. It was five minutes to five.

He reached out for the phone. 'Ahmed, I want you to pass the word that there will be a case meeting in the CID briefing room at 08.30 hours tomorrow morning. I want all the team there.'

'Right, sir.'

'And I still haven't seen DS Crisp, you know.'

'He's here now, sir,' Ahmed said.

Angel felt anger rise in his chest. 'Well tell him I want him in here.' He said and he banged the phone on to its cradle.

A few moments later, there was a knock at the door. 'Come in,' Angel roared.

It was Crisp. 'You wanted me, sir?'

Angel looked up. His jaw muscles tightened. 'This morning I wanted you. At this time, I am not so sure. Where the hell have you been? You are beginning to show me how easy it is to manage without you.'

Crisp looked closely into Angel's face, trying to judge how upset he was. Crisp reckoned he was pretty angry. He had to think quickly.

'Sorry, sir. Been pretty well tied up. Mrs Krill *didn't* go to see her daughter, you see. I have been trying to find out exactly where she *did* go.'

'*What* ?' Angel yelled. 'Why didn't you answer your mobile?'

'Didn't hear it, sir. Perhaps I was in a bad reception area. There are lots of tricky places like that in Sheffield.'

Angel didn't believe him but he did want to know about Kathleen Krill. 'Where was she Saturday night through to Sunday morning?'

'The time of her father's murder? I don't know yet, sir.'

Angel clenched his hands. 'When you find out, let me know. And when you're on duty *keep that mobile switched on*.'

'Oh yes, sir.'

'But before you get back to that, I have a little job for you.' He told him about the murder of Ingrid Underwood, the day's events and Ronnie Striker's unusual story. 'I simply want you to find the sandwich shop called *The Lunch Box*, it's round the corner from 221 Bradford Road. Check out whether the lad is telling the truth, that's all. Phone me on my mobile anytime tonight. I won't be getting home for a little while. And I want to see you in the CID briefing room here tomorrow morning at 8.30 sharp.'

'Right, sir.'

Crisp dashed off.

Angel reached out for the phone. He wanted to speak to his opposite number in the uniformed division, Inspector Haydn Asquith before he finished his shift.

'Yes, Michael, what can I do for you?'

'I need high-profile, twenty-four-hour cover on a murdered woman's house, Haydn. She was murdered in her shop this morning. I haven't a lead or a motive yet. There's possibly evidence in the house. SOCO will do a thorough search tomorrow. Understand she has family somewhere, but we haven't had the opportunity to follow that up. I was going along there now to see for myself. The address is 22 Park Road.'

'Leave it with me, Michael,' Asquith said. 'If anybody's been there or there's anything untoward, I'll get the lad to ring you on your mobile, if you like?'

Angel thanked him. He closed the phone, put it in his pocket, then he shuffled together the files and correspondence on his desk and shoved them into the middle drawer. He stood up and made for the door. Somebody knocked on it as he pulled it open. It was pretty DS Carter. They were both surprised.

'Find anything out?' Angel said.

'Nobody noticed anything, sir,' she said, 'except the man who has the bicycle shop right opposite, Carl Young.'

Angel sighed. 'I've already spoken to him at some length.'

Carter said, 'He said that Ronnie Striker was already sitting on the shop step when he arrived just before 8.30. He said that Ingrid arrived about a minute after he did.'

'He's certainly very interested in Ingrid Underwood's business.'

'I'd say he's got the hots for her,' she said with a smile.

Angel didn't smile. 'Aye, but did he see any *other* activity around the shop?'

'No sir. He said he was busy with a customer just after that.'

'So he didn't see Ronnie leave to fetch a sandwich, a man dressed like Jesus arrive, Ronnie return then run off, then the man dressed like Jesus leave and Miss Jubb, who found the body, arrive?'

'No, sir.'

He sniffed. 'Well, he missed a helluva lot, didn't he?'

'He said that he saw the marked car arrive at about 8.50.'

'That was pretty observant of him. A blind man on a galloping horse can see a police car half a mile away.'

Carter didn't know what to say.

'You asked down the road, didn't you?' Angel said. 'All the shops and offices and any place that had a direct line of sight of Ingrid Underwood's shop door?'

'Absolutely every one of them, sir.'

He wasn't pleased.

The phone rang. He snatched it up. It was Dr Mac.

'The woman was stabbed in the aorta, Michael. And a vicious wound it is. Made by the same dagger that was used to murder Luke Redman. I am afraid you have a serial killer on your hands.'

Angel took the news as confirmation of what he had already guessed. 'Aye,' he said. The worry is that if my understanding of the messages on the mirrors are to be understood, the murderer has said that there are now four more to die.'

'He's out of his mind,' Mac said, 'a lunatic. His MO, repetition of a theme, is bound to give him away.'

'How many of the four will he be successful in murdering before we catch him?'

'Well, you needn't spend any time looking for a laurel leaf, Michael.'

Angel blinked. 'Why?'

'Found one. It was tucked in the flap of her blouse.'

Angel swallowed.

Mac said, 'Speak to you tomorrow.'

'Aye. Thank you, Mac. Goodnight.'

He replaced the phone and looked up at Carter. 'That was Mac. Confirmation - if we had needed it - that we are looking for a serial killer.'

Carter's eyebrows shot up. She sucked in air as fast as a Maclaren.

*

Angel was pleased to be arriving home.

He drove the car into the garage, locked the door and made his way up the garden path. He looked at his watch. It was a quarter to seven. He usually arrived a few minutes past five. Mary would be waiting for him and she wouldn't be pleased. He knew he wasn't going to win a popularity contest.

He unlocked the back door as usual and went in.

Mary glared at him from the sitting room door and followed him through the kitchen to the hall wardrobe, her face as straight as a gun barrel.

'What time do you call this?' she said.

'Yes, love. I know I'm late,' he said as he took his coat off and put it on a coat hanger. 'I'm sorry.'

'Dinner's ruined. I don't know what I am going to give you. Whatever's happened?'

'It doesn't matter. I'll have...anything.'

She looked at him and stiffened. 'You won't have *anything*. You'll have a proper cooked meal, like all normal good-living people. What an outrageous thing to say, "I'll have anything." As if I would let you have any old thing that was...that was hanging around.'

'A corned beef sandwich would be fine,' he said shuffling into the sitting room.

'I haven't got any corned beef, and I wouldn't dream of giving you a sandwich for your main meal,' she said. Then she looked up as if inspired. 'Ah. I've got some eggs,' she said and rushed away into the kitchen.

Angel went to the end of sideboard and looked for the morning's post. That's where it was usually put, but there was nothing there.

'Any post?' he called.

'Nothing for you.'

He pulled a face then nodded. At least, no post meant there were no bills.

He meandered through into the kitchen. Mary was busy cracking eggs into a bowl. He opened the fridge, took out a bottle of German beer, knocked off the cap, poured it into a glass, made his way to the sitting room, sat down in his favourite chair, kicked of his shoes, loosened his tie, unfastened his top button and switched on the TV. As the set was warming up he heard Mary call out.

'Are you hungry?'

'Not really.'

'You'd better be,' she said, trying to sound threatening. His mobile phone rang. He fumbled around in his pocket for it.

Mary also heard the ring, groaned and muttered something.

Angel looked at the LCD. He saw that it was Crisp. 'Yes?' he said as he sat down in his favourite chair.

'I found the sandwich shop, *The Lunch Box*, sir. Ronnie Striker *did* go there this morning before nine. The woman who owns it said that she was not sure of the exact time. He ordered a sandwich that she prepared fresh. It took her only two minutes. And she understood that it was for Mrs Underwood. That's about it.'

'Did she say if he seemed agitated...did he behave any differently from normal, in any way?'

'No, sir. He wasn't a talker. Didn't have any social chit-chat. She knew *that*. So she didn't try. She said that she knew that he was...that there was something wrong with him.'

Angel's jaw muscles tightened. He squeezed the phone and put it closer to his mouth. 'The only thing that's wrong with the lad is that he has learning difficulties and has the mental age of a twelve-year-old. He's not...he's not *mad*.'

'I think she thought with me checking up on him that we had him down as a possible suspect. That's all.'

'Well, maybe she's wrong. Thank you, lad. Let's leave it there. Goodnight.'

He closed the phone. It rang again.

There were more groans from the kitchen. 'Don't be long on that thing,' she called. 'I'll be bringing your tea in shortly.'

Angel pressed the button. It was Police Constable Weightman. 'Sorry to bother you, sir, but I was instructed to give you a bell about the security of 22 Park Road.'

'Yes, John.'

'Seems all right, sir. Nobody here. No broken windows. Curtains open. No sign of a break in.'

'Right, John. Thank you. I hope you have a peaceful night.'

'Thank you, sir. Goodnight.'

He pocketed the phone as Mary appeared with a plate of scrambled eggs, toast and cutlery.

Neither spoke as they watched the news on the television. After the weather forecast, Mary found the TV remote and pressed a button. The screen went black.

Angel continued eating the scrambled eggs.

She was pleased that he was enjoying the makeshift meal. She sat in her chair the other side of the library table. 'What's happened, then?' she said.

'Nothing,' he said munching the last piece of toast.

'You're surely not late for no reason?'

'No, love.' He hesitated before he replied. He didn't want to alarm her unnecessarily. She would *have* to be told. He chewed and chewed then swallowed the last forkful of egg, then said, 'We've got a serial murderer, Mary. The same MO in the case of two deaths and there's the prospect of a further four more...unless we can catch him.'

Mary's face changed. Her mouth dropped open. A cold shiver ran up her back. 'Oh, Michael,' she said. 'How dreadful. You will be careful, won't you?'

*

It was 08.45 hours Thursday, 28 May, and Angel and his team were in the CID briefing room. Dr Mac was also there.

Angel was delivering a résumé of the two murder cases.

'DS Taylor advises us that as far as the scene is concerned,' Angel said, 'the murderer has shown himself to be forensically aware and, up to now, has left behind no clues that can be used to reveal his identity. Having said that, Dr Mac has found hairs on the body of Luke Redman which do not belong to him, and we are awaiting a DNA result from the lab at Wetherby. In the meantime, there are unusual questions to be addressed, such as why Ronnie Striker, a man who has a mental age of a 12-year-old, says that he saw Jesus on his knees at the side of Ingrid Underwood, and why the murderer apparently left a lone laurel leaf with the body of each victim.

'We have to work fast to make sure that the murderer doesn't strike for the third time. The matter paramount to the investigation now is to find the link between Luke Redman and Ingrid Underwood, and that is where our attention must be urgently directed. Any questions?'

A voice from the back said, 'From the wounds on both victims as described by Dr Mac, the murderer would be heavily marked with blood. Would the clothing thought to make the murderer look like Jesus be actually a sheet to save his own clothing being bloodstained underneath?'

Angel nodded. 'Could be. It's a valid suggestion that we must seriously consider, but it doesn't explain the sandals and the white star in Jesus's hand that Ronnie Striker says he saw.'

'There was a man in the market who has had bedsheets stolen from his stall, sir,' Crisp said.

'Must be followed up,' Angel said. 'I'll leave that with you, Trevor, but our priority at this juncture has to be to find the link between Luke Redman and Ingrid Underwood. That would hopefully lead to avoiding any of the four other deaths the murderer has threatened.'

'If it was a sheet, sir,' the voice at the back said, 'the murderer would need to destroy the bloodstained sheet, wouldn't he? The thorough murderer would burn or bury it. There's no other absolute way.'

'That's right,' Angel said.

'I was thinking that recently turned-over earth or a fire somewhere -'

'That's right, and if anybody comes across such indications in the course of their inquiries, they should follow it up. But, I bring you all back to it, nothing is more important than finding that link. Anything else?'

'A laurel leaf wreath is, of course, made of laurel leaves, sir,' Carter said. 'And a laurel wreath is what they used to hang round racing drivers who have won the Grand Prix, and statues of famous men on their anniversaries and so on. Is there a link between some famous race or event and the two victims?'

Angel nodded. 'I don't know, lass. Can't think of anything off hand. That's what we have to find out.' He looked up and across the eager faces. 'Anything else?'

Nobody seemed to have anything more to say.

'Right,' Angel said. 'Thank you all very much. Please carry on. Will DS Carter and DS Crisp and DC Scrivens see me in my office straightaway?'

CHAPTER SIX

'Come in, all of you,' Angel said. 'Shut the door. I see you've met DS Carter.'

Scrivens said, 'Yes, sir.'

Crisp grinned. 'Yes, sir.'

Carter smiled across at Crisp.

Angel noticed the glance and thought they must like each other. He didn't like it. He hoped it wouldn't develop into some sort of romance.

He looked at her and said, 'You have to report on Cyril Krill.'

Carter's eyes flashed. 'I haven't had the opportunity before, sir.'

'I know you haven't,' Angel said. 'You've got it now. Tell me about him.'

'It's all a bit odd, sir,' she said. 'Everybody says Cyril Krill is in a financial mess. He was doing very well until about six months ago. Last year's bank and house price collapse seems to have left him in financial straits. As far as I can find out, he has no building projects in hand. All his builders and plasterers and joiners were employed on a contract basis and they have been dismissed. But the Krills still live in a big house in Sheffield, and both he and his wife have big cars. And they went to that trade fair in London together.'

Angel turned to Crisp. 'I thought his wife went somewhere to see their daughter.'

'She wasn't at her school in Gloucestershire, as she said,' Crisp said. 'She could have done, sir.'

'Why would she lie about that?' Angel said looking round. Nobody offered an explanation.

'The headmistress said that she was expected,' Crisp said, 'but at the last minute phoned and said she wasn't feeling well. The daughter was apparently very disappointed.'

'If she was *not* well enough to see her daughter, how come she was well enough to go to London with her husband?' Angel said. He looked at Crisp. 'I really need to know where the Krills were at the time of her father's murder and at the time of Ingrid Underwood's murder.'

'Right, sir,' Crisp said, and made for the door.

'Wait a couple of minutes for me. I'll come with you. It's the only lead we've got.'

'Right, sir,' Crisp said. 'My car's out at the front,' he added and went out.

Angel turned to Scrivens. 'You were looking into the possibility that Luke Redman might have made an enemy at his work.'

'Yes, sir,' Scrivens said. 'Mr Redman only ever worked at the Northern Bank. I called on the few contemporaries still living, and made several phone calls, sir. And nobody thought he was that bad...I mean bad enough for anyone to want to murder him. He wouldn't have won any popularity contest, but as bank managers go, it seems he was pretty straight.'

'All right, Ted. I hope you're right,' Angel said and rubbed his chin. 'There are a couple of details you can clear up for me. You know that Ronnie Striker went out to buy a sandwich from the shop for Ingrid Underwood. We know he bought the thing. Presumably he brought it back to the florist's shop but there was no explanation as to what happened to it. Even in the clear-up, SOCO didn't come across it. I want you to find out what happened to it. See Ronnie Striker; he should know, but be gentle, don't upset him. Remember he has a man's body but he's only twelve years old in the head. All right?'

'Yes, sir.'

'And there's something else. Go to the florist's shop. SOCO will soon be finished there. Find out about the shop bell, and report back to me how it works.'

Scrivens frowned. 'The shop bell, sir?'

Angel clenched his fists. 'Yes,' he said. 'The shop bell. How is it powered? Electric mains, battery, gas, oil, solar, steam, coal, gravity...or is it simply a bell suspended and hit by a piece of metal screwed to the door when the door is opened.'

Scrivens' face lightened. 'Oh, yes, sir.'

'Well, push off then, lad,' he said. 'We are working against the clock here, you know. I don't want the murderer striking a third time.'

Scrivens' eyelids shot up and then down in alarm as the possibility dawned on him. He rushed out and closed the door.

Angel turned to Carter. 'Now then, lass. The link between Luke Redman and Ingrid Underwood has to be much more than him buying flowers from her shop from time to time, or her being a customer at the bank when he was manager, although they are obviously places where a connection may have started. We have to find the relations, friends and acquaintances of each of the two victims and from them, try to uncover a situation or circumstance they had in common. Whatever it is, it must be able to be incorporated in some way with another four people, because the murderer has signalled that he intends to kill four more.'

'Why six?'

'Who knows? It doesn't fit a team number, does it? I don't know of any particular group that would make six. Or it could be seven if you included the murderer.'

'There's seven-a-side football, sir.'

‘I can’t see Redman in a football team with Mrs Underwood. There’s more than twenty-five years’ difference in them for one thing.’

Carter had to agree. She nodded accordingly.

‘I don’t know why it’s six, lass,’ Angel said. ‘But it is. We know so little about Ingrid Underwood. The man across the road at the bike shop said she has a daughter but she’s not come forward. Start there. There should be an address book or some clue as to her ID in Ingrid Underwood’s house. See what you can do to find her or any other person close to her. Keep in touch. All right?’

‘Right sir,’ she said and she was gone.

Angel looked round the empty office, checked that he had everything he needed, then went out, closed the door, ran up the corridor to the front door of the station to join Crisp who was already in his car, his engine running, waiting for him.

Angel slumped in the passenger seat, dragged the seat-belt across his chest, pressed the metal bit into the fastener, and signalled Crisp to move off.

It was not a happy day.

They travelled in silence. Angel used the time to mull over the case and then marshal the questions he had for the Krills.

Crisp drove the Ford to Sheffield, and then through the twists and turns of the city-centre streets with their ‘No Entry’, ‘No right turn’, ‘No left turn’ signs and with certain roads restricted to buses and taxis only. He found the way on to Rivelin Valley Road, then on to the A57 Manchester Road towards the Peak District National Park. Among a stretch of architect designed houses on the right hand side was the house of Cyril and Kathleen Krill.

Mrs Krill answered the door.

Angel sensed that they were about as welcome as a gas bill. She showed them into the drawing room.

After preliminaries, which were kept to a minimum, Angel said, ‘Your husband not here?’

'Oh yes,' she said. 'He's in his office which is an annexe at the rear of the house. Do you wish me to call him?' she said reaching for the phone.

'Not yet,' he said. 'I need to know where you were overnight on Saturday night/Sunday morning last and between 8.40 and 9.00 yesterday morning.'

'I have already told you that I was at my daughter's school on Saturday night.'

Angel looked at Crisp.

Crisp said, 'The headmistress says that you phoned her on Saturday morning and said that you had a migraine and that -'

She glared at Angel. 'You've been checking up on me.'

'Of course,' Angel said.

'Do you think I would want to kill my own father?'

Angel shrugged. 'I don't know you, Mrs Krill. I am only a policeman doing a very unpleasant job. Can you simply answer the question?'

She licked her top lip with the tip of her tongue, thoughtfully. 'It was true,' she said. 'I did have a migraine, so I stayed at home. I was in bed most of the time.'

Angel blinked, looked at Crisp who was getting ready to speak, held up his hand to stop him and said, 'Here, in this house alone, the entire weekend?'

'Yes,' she said.

'And I don't suppose you saw anybody throughout that time.'

Her lips tightened. 'You can't see anything, Inspector, when you have a serious attack. Ask any doctor.'

Angel sighed. 'So nobody can vouch for you being here?'

'No.'

'Why did you say you went to see your daughter? It would have been perfectly simple to have told the truth.'

Her eyes darted to the left to the right and back again. 'Oh for god's sake, I lied. My husband was there. He thought my migraines had gone. I didn't want him to think I was still suffering from them. He has enough to worry about just now. It was easier to tell a white lie than to explain.'

Angel frowned. He wasn't satisfied, but time was precious. Wherever she was, she hadn't an alibi for the time of her father's murder.

'And where were you yesterday morning?' he said.

'I was here. Why?'

'Can anybody corroborate that?'

'My husband, I suppose. He was in his office...like he is now. Why?'

'Because that was the time a woman in a flower shop, a Mrs Ingrid Underwood, was stabbed to death the same way that your father was killed. And a similar message left on a mirror.'

'Oh, my god,' she said and slumped down in a chair. 'What did it say?'

'"IV to go," which we believe to mean that the murderer intends to kill four more people.'

'Good heavens,' Mrs Krill said.

'Do you know if your father knew Mrs Underwood?'

'Poor woman. I have no idea. The name doesn't sound familiar. Although he may have.'

'It's very important. He never spoke of her? Never bought flowers from her? It's an unusual name.'

'No, Inspector. I can't recall the name.'

'Can you tell me who formed your father's circle of friends, relations and acquaintances?'

'That's not difficult, Inspector. There was only me. He had had a wide range of interests when he was younger and when he was working. And he had tried to maintain them, but I believe his particular circle died off, or moved into nursing or retirement homes or even emigrated to a warmer climate. After my mother died, he lost interest in most things. Lately he only went out of the house to the supermarket, the post office and the doctor's surgery.'

'What about relatives?'

'They never visited.'

'Neighbours?'

'Oooh yes. The next door neighbour...he used to talk to a lot. She seemed a nice lady...a widow, on her own. Mrs Oxtaby.'

'Mrs Oxtaby?' Angel said. 'She's been seen, but we'll have another word. Anybody else?'

'No. I'm afraid that was the extent of Dad's social life these recent days.'

Angel wrinkled his nose. He lifted his eyebrows and looked at Crisp who shook his head very slightly. He turned back to Mrs Krill. 'Right. Thank you. I'd like to see your husband now.'

She looked up and said, 'Is that all?'

'Yes. For now.'

She picked up the phone, told her husband that the police wanted to see him, then directed the two men down the hall, out through the back door and down a path through a lawn to a bungalow. Krill came out of the building and stood in front of the door as they approached.

'What do you want?' he said. 'Have you come to tell me who murdered old man Redman, then?'

Angel said, 'Do you think we could talk inside, sir?'

Krill hesitated then moved away from the door and said, 'You'll have to make it quick. I haven't much time.'

'Nor have we,' Angel said and he passed in front of him, stepped into the bungalow and made for the only room ahead with the door open.

Crisp followed.

Krill brought up the rear, closed the door, stepped behind a desk, pointed to chairs facing him and the three men sat down.

Angel got straight down to business. 'You went down to London to an exhibition? You stayed there on Saturday night?'

'Yes. What about it?' Krill said.

'The exhibition organizer said that you went with your wife.'

'So what?'

'Your wife says that she spent the weekend in the house alone.'

Krill breathed in quickly and rubbed his chin. 'The organizer doesn't know my wife. He's obviously confused.'

'It wasn't the organizer who wrote Mr and Mrs Cyril Krill in the visitor's book, sir. *It was you.*'

'Did I? Did I really? You have been busy little boys. Slip of the pen, I expect. I had a thousand things on my mind. It's something you do automatically...it's of no importance.'

'Normally it may have been of no importance, but on this occasion I need to know where you were overnight.'

'In London.'

'You didn't return home, where did you stay?'

'I don't remember now...there are...places.'

Angel's jaw muscles hardened. 'I need to know where you were, sir.'

Krill glared back at him. 'I don't know exactly. There are places where you can drink all night and...relax...and enjoy yourself.'

'Where, Mr Krill? For your sake, you may need to know *exactly* where?'

Krill shook his head. 'I was having a drink in a cocktail bar called the Mediterranean on Winter Street, and this girl came in. Very attractive. We got talking. Her name was Marilyn...or Madelaine...or something; anyway she said she knew a great new nightclub just opened, so we went there. It was a small restaurant with singing and dancing. We had a table at the front. We had a few drinks and watched the floor show. I was having a great time. But I don't remember much after that. I may have been drugged. We went back to her place, I think, or somewhere. I don't know where it was. I remember waking up, on the Embankment, hanging on to a lamppost, being sick over a grate. I had a raging headache. All the cash had gone from my wallet and my watch had been taken. I still had my credit card and my overnight bag. That's all I remember.'

Angel rubbed his chin. 'Did you pay for anything with your credit card or by cheque?'

'Nightclubs and bars only take cash. They took *all* of mine.'

Angel shook his head. Unless the girl could be traced and her evidence accepted, there was no alibi there. 'What about yesterday morning between 8.40 and 9.00?'

'I was here. Working in this office, why?'

Angel noted that that at least was in accord with his wife's reply, unless she was covering for him. He must move on.

'A woman was murdered. A florist. Mrs Ingrid Underwood. Did you know her? Please think about the name before you answer.'

'Ingrid Underwood? Never heard of her.'

Angel wondered whether to believe him. Time was short. 'You didn't get along with your father-in-law. Did you?'

Krill looked surprised. He didn't answer straightaway. He thought about it a few moments then said, 'Luke Redman was all right. I didn't really have anything to do with him latterly. In fact, I haven't seen him for ages...not since his wife's funeral. That was three years ago. My wife visited him three or four times a week, and ran about after him, and put up with his moods and tantrums. She played the perfect daughter to the end. I didn't mind that she did that. I didn't attempt to stop her.'

'Was he a good father-in-law? Did he help you when you were young? Financially?'

'He got us a mortgage at a lower than average interest rate through the Northern Bank.'

That would have been a help, Angel thought.

Then Krill said, 'The day I married Kathleen, he said he would always be happy to consider any loan secured by bricks and mortar at a better than competitive rate. I thought that was the least he could have done for his daughter and son-in-law. Anyway, in 2004, I approached him with a proposal.

It took him a couple of days to give me a quote. It was good. His branch of the Northern Bank loaned me a million and a quarter to enable me to buy a five-bedroomed house with three acres of land and outline planning permission for two detached houses.'

Angel nodded. That sounded good.

The corners of Krill's mouth turned down. 'Then four months later, when the houses were half built and I hadn't made a sale of either of them, he foreclosed. He was concerned that the Northern Bank wouldn't get their money back. I had four days in which to get refinanced.'

'You got out all right?' Angel said.

'In the end, yes. It was touch and go for a while. Of course, the emergency refinancing cost a pretty penny and took the profit off the deal. So thereafter, I vowed to give Luke Redman a very wide berth.'

'How's the property developing business now?'

'Patchy,' Krill said. 'I do all right,' he added.

'A reliable little birdie told me that you were experiencing serious financial difficulties.'

'If I knew the name of your reliable little birdie I would sue it for slander.'

CHAPTER SEVEN

Angel considered that he could not make any more progress with Cyril Krill. He ended the interview and he and Crisp returned to the car.

When Crisp had negotiated the Ford through the Sheffield city centre and was on the Bromersley Road, Angel said, 'You know, Luke Redman must have left a tidy sum to his daughter, and some of it will no doubt trickle down to Cyril Krill, so it wouldn't be difficult to construct a motive for his murder of the old man. And if Krill cannot find a believable witness to support his whereabouts on the night of the murder, we may also have him for opportunity. He could easily have left London by car or train in the evening, committed the murder and returned to London overnight.'

'Yes, sir. If you could make it stick, all you would need is the means.'

'Hmm. But what about the murder of Ingrid Underwood? Kathleen Krill says they were together in the house at the time.'

'She could be covering for him if they were in this together.'

'Yes. But there's no motive we know of, and we still don't have the means.'

'That's true, sir. Shouldn't we search the house?'

'We should,' Angel said pursing his lips. 'But we do not have the time. Even if we searched Krill's house, if he was guilty, I think he would be too smart to leave a dagger about the place.'

'Or a blood-soaked cloak or blanket or sheet.'

'Hmm. Finding the link between old man Redman and the florist is our best defence against a third victim. And, as a matter of urgency, when we get back, I want you to visit the supermarket, the post office, the doctor's surgery and Mrs Oxtaby's and see if you can dig up a connection between the two.'

Angel's mobile rang. It was Scrivens.

'I saw Ronnie Striker and his mother, sir. He said he put the sandwich in his pocket in the sandwich shop. He said that he ran all the way home with it still in his pocket. He didn't realize he had brought it home until he took his coat off. He ate it later. It would have gone dry. His mother said she would happily pay for it, if necessary.'

Angel nodded. 'And what about the shop doorbell?'

'It's electric, sir,' Scrivens said. 'It rings immediately the door is opened but stops as it is pushed further open. It also rings again as the door is almost closed until it is completely shut.'

'So it is entirely consistent with Striker's evidence, that when he returned from the sandwich shop, the door was propped open with a brick?'

'Yes, sir.'

Angel wasn't surprised, but it had needed clarifying. 'And when the murderer left the scene, he must have removed the brick to permit the door to close, because that's how the old lady, Mrs Jubb had found it.'

'Looks like it, sir.'

'Right. Now there's another little job for you. I want you to find out if Ingrid Underwood banks, or has ever banked, at the Northern Bank.'

'Right, sir.'

Angel closed his phone and dropped it into his pocket. Soon afterwards, he saw the road speed restriction signs and the boundary sign showing they were on the outskirts of Bromersley.

'Drop me off at Luke Redman's house,' Angel said.

Three minutes later, Crisp turned the Ford left on to Creesforth Road and up to the front gate of number 14.

As Angel got out of the car, he said, 'Ta, lad. Now crack on with those inquiries. And don't mess about. At this very moment I expect the murderer is almost certainly planning or even executing a third murder.'

The thought made Crisp sigh, and his eyes glowed for a moment. 'Right, sir,' he said as he released the handbrake and drove away.

Angel opened the gate and walked down the drive. The policeman was standing at the door. He threw up a salute.

'Good morning,' Angel said. 'Anybody inside?'

'No, sir. It's all very quiet.'

Angel nodded and walked into the hall. He made straight to the study where Luke Redman had a hundred or more framed photographs on the walls illustrating the many activities he had been involved in over a long and busy life. Each picture was carefully, neatly captioned in giving names, date, place and occasion. Angel found the photographs fascinating because some were clearly taken when Redman was only an infant. He looked at one particular one. He thought it was the oldest there. Young Luke was standing against a broken-down fence in a small backyard in short trousers with three bewhiskered men in dark suit trousers held up with leather braces, spotless white shirts without collars and heavy shoes or boots standing behind him. The caption read, 'Dad, Grandad, Great Grandad and me. 113 Railway Terrace, Ratton, Bromersley, 1931'.

Angel rubbed his chin. He knew that Ratton had been and still was a deprived area of Bromersley. It was supposed to have been overrun with rats, hence the name. Nobody liked to admit that they originated from there or that they lived there.

He moved along passing the gallery of photographs depicting Luke Redman's history and he glanced at them again. The pictures seemed endless. He lingered over the formal photographs showing Redman taking part in local stage productions of *The Gondoliers*, *Nero*, *The Importance of Being Ernest*. It was just at that point that Angel went back to the photograph of *Nero*. He peered at it carefully. It was a photograph of the cast and production team. Three men were in formal evening dress. The other eighteen men and women were in stage costumes comprising Roman toga-type robes and sandals. One of the younger men was wearing a headpiece made from laurel leaves. He read the caption. '*Nero*. Entire cast, director, stage manager and prompt (guide on back of photograph). Dress rehearsal. Victorian Theatre, May 1989.'

Angel suddenly became aware of a thumping sensation under his shirt. He could hear the beat in his ears. His face was hot.

His eyes quickly scanned the photograph of the people in early Roman dress. He soon picked out the unmistakable features of Luke Redman and then feverishly began to look for Ingrid Underwood. There were two women it could have been. There was a beautiful woman who would have been aged about thirty. Then he was certain. One of them looked exactly, certainly, undoubtedly, positively like Ingrid Underwood.

His blood ran cold. His heart was pumping 180 or more to the minute.

There were too many indicators for him to be mistaken. It was all there. White togas, sandals, laurel leaves, Luke Redman and Ingrid Underwood.

He unhooked the photograph from the wall. He nearly dropped it. His fingers were like jelly. He placed it on Redman's desk. And looked at it again. He wanted to be absolutely sure.

There were twenty-one people on the photograph, two of them were dead and four had been condemned to death.

What about the other fifteen? Why were four more chosen to be murdered? And which four were they? If he knew that, he could warn them against the murderer. One of nineteen was probably the murderer. The photograph was dated May 1989. It was the twenty-year anniversary. Maybe something that happened twenty years ago was the cause of the murders.

He turned the photograph over. The back of the frame was neatly and efficiently sealed with lengths of brown paper sticky tape. He took out his pearl-handled fruit knife, stabbed it into the paper, peeled some of it away, removed the plywood back, took out the photograph and a piece of tracing paper the same size as the photograph which had outline drawings of each person's head and shoulders with their name neatly printed on it. He read them all quickly to see if he recognized any of the names. Luke Redman and Ingrid Underwood were the only two he knew. The muscles round his mouth tightened. He blew out air, pulled out his mobile and quickly tapped in a number. It was soon answered by Ahmed.

'I want you to get DS Crisp, DS Carter, DC Scrivens and yourself in my office ASAP for a case conference,' he said. 'I'll be there in about seven minutes. Also, I want you to put this next part of this phone call on to record, to save time. All right?'

'It *is* already recording, sir,' Ahmed said.

Angel blinked. He was surprised. 'Right,' he said. 'Well, I have a list of nineteen people's names, and four of them are at risk of being murdered at any moment, so we have to find them very quickly. I want you to tap them into that computer of yours and print it out smartish. All right? I'm going to read them out. Are you ready?'

'Go ahead, sir.'

*

Angel arrived back at the station six minutes later. He rushed past the cells and charged up the green corridor into the CID room. Ahmed was standing by the computer printer near the door. A sheet of A4 paper shot out on to the tray. He leaned forward and picked it up.

Angel snatched it from him. 'This the list?'

'Yes, sir.'

'Print six more, and bring them through,' he said. 'Anybody arrived?'

'Flora Carter, and Ted Scrivens are in your -'

Angel interrupted him. 'Just a minute, lad. Who told you that you could call Detective Sergeant Carter by her first name?'

Ahmed looked up innocently. 'She doesn't mind, sir,' he said.

Angel's lips tightened. '*She* may not mind, lad. But *I* do. In my hearing, you refer to her as DS Carter or Sergeant Carter. All right?'

Ahmed stared at Angel with his mouth open. He wanted to reply, but he couldn't.

'Now, I was asking you,' Angel said, 'where *is* everybody?'

'DS Carter and DC Scrivens are in your office, sir, and DS Crisp is on his way.'

Angel grunted and dashed out looking down the list.

Crisp arrived at the office as Angel opened the door. Ahmed followed on seconds later with more copies which he handed to Angel.

When they were assembled, Angel told them about finding the photograph and how he believed it all fitted together. He then showed them the photograph.

'There are twenty-one people in total,' he said. 'We know that two of them are dead so we need to find the remaining nineteen to warn them that there is a possibility that they might be one of the four we know the murderer intends to kill.'

Carter said, 'Isn't it possible, sir, that the murderer is one of the nineteen?'

'I think it is almost certain that he is, Sergeant, so I want you to be very careful when you are interviewing any of them by yourselves, on their turf. Better to get them to come to the station, if it's practical. We will send a car, if there's one available. Specifically at this moment, our job is to save lives. There are five of us, so for speed I propose that we divide the nineteen among us, that's only three or four each. Any questions?'

Ahmed said, 'As one of them *is* the murderer, sir, and we're warning *him*, he'll know that we are warning everybody else, won't he?'

'I know it is bizarre, Ahmed, but that's the way it has to be. Our priority is to stop the murderer, whoever he is, from murdering anybody else,' Angel said. 'Now let's press on with it. Seconds may be precious. The list is twenty years old, and there aren't any addresses, so it may not be straightforward.'

There were mutters of general understanding and uneasiness.

Angel handed out the lists. 'I'll take the top three. Crisp take the next four, Carter the next four, then Ted Scrivens four, then Ahmed, the last four. That's nineteen. That's the lot. All right?'

There were mutters of, 'Yes, sir,' as they rushed for the door.

'And no fighting over the phone book,' he called out, 'there's more than one copy in the station.'

*

By six o'clock that afternoon, the team had discovered that fifteen of the remaining nineteen on the photograph had died naturally over the past twenty years. The identity and location of each death (mostly Bromersley General Hospital) had been confirmed by the Births, Deaths and Marriages office in Bromersley Town Hall. That left only four persons, three men and one woman, still alive.

DS Crisp had discovered that Tom Franks was one of the men and was working at Cheapo's supermarket. He was manager of the fruit and vegetable section. It was a name on

Crisp's list so he had made a beeline straight to the supermarket and persuaded him to come back to the station to help the police with their inquiries.

It was 7.15 p.m. when Crisp showed him into Interview Room No. 1, where Angel was waiting for him.

'Come in, Mr Franks. Sorry to drag you away from your work.'

He was a chubby, sweaty man who seemed confused by the unusual situation he seemed to be in.

Crisp closed the door.

'Please sit down. Has the sergeant told you why we want you here?'

'That I might be in danger. Something to do with that *Nero* play that I was in years back.'

'*Exactly* twenty years ago, Mr Franks.'

'Really? Twenty years is it? I thought it was a bit of a coincidence that Lance Redman *and* Ingrid Underwood...I saw it in *The Chronicle*...who both had leading parts in the play, should have been murdered this week. I had been thinking about it. It brought it all back to me. The tragedy of it all.'

'Tragedy? What tragedy?'

'The death of young Malcolm Malloy. Nice lad. Destined for big things. Another Richard Burton. Malcolm was the worst injured in the fire. He was so badly burned he eventually died in the burns unit.'

Angel rubbed his chin. 'Really. A fire? What happened?'

'The play only ran for the one night. There was a fire on the stage. It was Malcolm's fault. But it was an accident. He was badly burned.'

Angel frowned. 'Anybody else injured?'

'Several, but nothing serious.'

'Do you think his death has any bearing on the deaths of Lance Redman and Ingrid Underwood? And posed a threat to the rest of the cast? We were hopeful that you might throw some light on their deaths. You see, somebody is deliberately, systematically, intending to eliminate all the people who had been connected with that play.'

Franks frowned and looked into Angel's eyes. He said nothing.

'Have you any idea who it is and why?' Angel said.

'No. No idea. Why would anybody want to do that?'

'Is there any significance in the order that they were murdered, Lancelot Redman first and then Ingrid Underwood?'

'Not unless it's age. Lancelot would have been the oldest member of the Bromersley Players, I think. He played Seneca, a sort of wise man who advised Nero. But no. Ingrid would not have been the second oldest. I think she played one of Nero's sisters...or it could have been Messalina. I can't remember all the names now.'

'The thing is, Mr Franks, you are in grave danger. You are one of only four people from the production of that play who is still alive. The murderer knows that, and he has indicated that he intends to murder all four.'

'I don't understand. How do you know all this?'

'That is something I need, at this stage, to keep confidential.'

'Oh? Yes. Well, that's quite...alarming, Inspector.'

'That's why I want you here in protective custody.'

'You mean, here...locked in a cell?' He rubbed his face and began to perspire profusely. He wiped his neck with his handkerchief.

'Well, only locked in with your permission, sir. For your own safety. You can come out anytime provided that you are suitably escorted.'

'How long for?'

'Until we find the murderer.'

'What about my wife and kids?'

'We have no reason to think that they are in any danger at all. They can visit you, and you can talk to them or anybody else anytime on the phone.'

He nodded, then shrugged. 'I don't seem to have much choice. Who are the other three? Where are they?'

'We are still searching for them. They'll be afforded the same protection as you.'

Angel looked across at Crisp. The sergeant here will fix you up in a cell for the night, Mr Franks. Anything you need, please liaise with him. All right?'

Franks nodded and blinked several times.

Crisp led him out of the office.

Franks looked as if he'd been battered with a barrister's briefcase.

Once on his own, Angel rubbed his chin and wondered why he'd stopped smoking. He sat quietly in the swivel chair, pushed it backwards and looked up at the ceiling. He stayed there for a few minutes gazing at the dirty ring mark round the ceiling rose, then suddenly he rocked forward, leaped out of the chair and out of the office.

CHAPTER EIGHT

It was eight o'clock that Thursday evening when Angel brought his car to a stop with a squeal of brakes outside *The Bromersley Chronicle* office. He dashed up to the front doors. They were locked and a sign up said CLOSED. He wasn't surprised.

He dashed down a ginnel at the side of the old stone building, on to the car park, past a pile of wooden crates containing huge rolls of newsprint, through the rear loading door, through the noisy printing room down a corridor to offices at the end. He found a young woman running along the corridor with some newspaper pages in her hand.

She looked at him in surprise.

'I am Detective Inspector Angel; can I see Mr Keene urgently, please?'

She pointed towards an open door. It was the editor's office.

The big man was standing over his desk, his shirt sleeves rolled up. 'Not often I see you here, Inspector,' Keene said. 'Especially at this time of night. What's up?'

'I need your help, sir.'

'Well, I'm a bit pushed just now. It's publication day tomorrow, you know. But what is it? I always do everything I can to help the police. You know that.'

He nodded. 'You keep records of back copies of *The Chronicle*?'

'Yep. On computer now, Inspector. In the early days, we used to keep the actual newspaper. Everything now brought up to date. The actual paper is photographed. How far back do you want to go?'

'Twenty years.'

The editor's bushy eyebrows shot up. 'Really? That shouldn't be difficult.' He reached out and with great deliberation pressed a button on his desk.

'I am looking for information about a play that was being performed at the Variety Theatre,' Angel said.

'I'll get my man in to sort it out for you, Inspector. Seeing that it is you, I expect it's something to do with those other murders we reported last week.'

Angel sniffed. 'Could be. Could be,' he said.

The editor smiled knowingly. 'When you get him, don't forget us, Inspector. *The Chronicle* likes to be *first* with all local news.'

Through the open door a tall skinny man appeared. He looked across at Angel then at the editor.

The editor stood up. 'Inspector, this is Jack Hanger. Jack, this is the famous Inspector Angel. Jack keeps the records up to date and is a whiz on the computer. Please look after the Inspector, Jack. He wants to make use of our records, and he's promised to give us a good story...eventually.'

'Right, boss,' Hanger said.

'Assist him in any way he wants,' Keene added. 'I must get on. If you'll excuse me, Inspector, I have a paper to put to bed.'

He dashed out.

Hanger led the way out of the editor's grand office to a tiny room with a trestle table covered in newsprint. There was a computer keyboard, a large screen at the far end of the table, and two chairs.

'I'm proofreader as well as everything else. What is it you want exactly, Inspector?' Hanger said as he pulled up a chair to the computer and tapped a few keys on the keyboard causing the screen to change.

Angel sat next to him and said, ‘In May 1989 there was a play performed at the Variety Theatre. It used to be on Barnsley Road. I believe it is now closed down. The play was called *Nero*. I want to know what you’ve got on it. There would probably be advertisements ahead of it, to sell tickets, and there might have been a write-up about it afterwards.’

Hanger nodded, tapped a few keys and up came a picture of the front page of *The Chronicle* dated 18 May 1989.

‘Is that it?’ Hanger said.

Angel nodded appreciatively and leaned eagerly forward. It read:

*

VARIETY THEATRE CLOSED FOLLOWING FIRE.
NERO STAR, MALCOLM MALLOY BADLY
INJURED.

A fire broke out on the stage during the first night of the Bromersley Players’ production of *Nero*.

The up-and-coming local star, Malcolm Malloy, 25, was severely burned and rushed by ambulance to Bromersley General.

This production of the play *Nero* had to be cancelled.

Most of the scenery, the flies and the dressing rooms were damaged. The safety curtain saved the rest of the theatre. None of the 850 audience was affected apart from a small amount of smoke.

The fire started during the last act, which depicted the burning of Rome, as Nero, played by Malloy, ‘fiddled’ while the city burned.

Malloy was later transferred to the specialist burns unit. Several other members of the cast were also treated for minor burns.

Arrangements for the refund of ticket money are already in hand.

In the Variety Theatre's 110-year history there has never been a fire of this magnitude.

The play's director, Jonathan Parker-Snell, said, 'It was a great tragedy that Malcolm Malloy should have been injured. He had had a promising career since leaving RADA, taking several leading roles locally, including the leading role in *Romeo and Juliet* at the Little Plumm Theatre in Hemingfield, near Barnsley. Also, I am extremely disappointed that the play has to be cancelled, after all the hard work the cast has put into it, but under the circumstances it is unavoidable.'

The fire was thought to have been caused by a faulty oxygen line. To represent the fire scene, metal troughs containing special flammable substances were placed strategically around the stage, concealed by scenery. On cue, these were remotely ignited by the props manager, Mr Dennis Long. The height and ferocity of the flames of each trough was individually controlled by pumping oxygen into the flame. One of the pump's valves appeared to have blown open as the character, Nero, played by the star, Malcolm Malloy, who also ventured too close, caught his costume in the flame-producing apparatus. Malloy was unable to free his costume and in the attempt to escape, he pulled the pipe across himself and was very badly burned on the face, chest, arms and stomach. The flames also spread to the scenery. Several of the cast and the stage manager, Charles Catchpole, tried to detach the pipe from Malloy and received minor injuries in the process. Eventually the safety curtain was lowered, the fire department arrived and the fire was quickly extinguished.

*

Angel read the text again. His eyes were glowing, his heart thumping. This was the breakthrough he had been longing for.

He turned to Hanger and said, 'Can I have a copy of this?'

'Of course.'

The clerk pressed some keys and a printed copy shot out on to the tray. Angel reached out for it.

'If there's anything else you want, Inspector?'

Angel was deep in thought. He looked up. 'No thank you, Mr Hanger. That's a big help.'

'If there's anything else you need, come straight to me. The boss said I was to help you all I could.'

Angel nodded and, holding on to the print, he ran out of the little office, through the printing room, out of the back door, where vans were being loaded with newspapers, and up the ginnel back to the BMW.

*

Five minutes later, at 20.45 hours, Angel arrived back at the police station.

Ahmed saw him pass the CID office door and he dashed out in the corridor to speak to him. 'Sir.'

Angel heard him, stopped and turned.

'DS Crisp has located the Margaret Ireland on his list,' Ahmed said: 'She lives on Wakefield Road. And he's gone out to bring her in.'

Angel's face brightened. 'That's great, lad.'

He rubbed his chin and proceeded towards his office. That meant that there were only two more to find. Then he suddenly stopped, turned back and said, 'Has he gone on his own?'

'Yes, sir.'

Angel's lips tightened back against his teeth simultaneously sucking in air and making a hissing noise. Although he had thought all along that the murders had been executed by a member of the male gender, nevertheless the murderer *could* have been a woman, and *that* woman could have been Miss Margaret Ireland.

'How long has he been gone?'

'About ten minutes, sir.'

He sighed. 'Let me know the moment they arrive.'

'Yes, sir,' Ahmed said. 'And there's another man, Kenneth Lamb.'

Angel turned round again. 'Yes, lad? What about him?'

'He is on my list. I've just tracked him down on the phone, sir. I told him that his life was possibly in danger. He didn't take it seriously. I asked him to stay where he was, to lock the house up and we would send a car for him. He laughed at the idea and said that he *might* come here himself when he'd had his tea.'

Angel's fists tightened. 'Have you got his address?'

'Yes, sir.'

'Come in the office.' He reached the desk, picked up the phone and handed it to him. 'Tell Transport I want a vehicle urgently now to collect you, pick this joker up at his place and bring you both back here *smartly*. All right?'

Ahmed blinked, took the phone and began tapping in the internal number 4 for Transport.

Scrivens came through the open office door.

Angel looked up. 'What are you busy with?'

'Angus Peel, sir.'

'Ah, the last one.'

'Yes, sir.'

'Have you found him?'

'No, sir.'

The team had found out that he worked as a stairlift installer, deliveryman and was assistant manager of a local shop that sold mobility aids to the disabled and old people.

'He must be somewhere,' Angel said.

'He installed a stairlift at a house in Wombwell this afternoon, sir,' Scrivens said.

'Have you checked that?'

'I haven't, sir, but Flora has. She's actually -'

Angel said, 'Just a minute lad. Just a minute. Who is this Flora you're talking about?'

'Oh,' he said. He remembered that Angel would not approve of him referring to the sergeant by her first name.

'I mean DS Carter, sir.'

'Aye. That's better. Carry on. What were you saying?'

'That DS Carter has been to Wombwell and spoken to the householder.'

Angel sighed. 'Go find her for me.'

Carter appeared at the door. 'You looking for me, sir?'

'Aye. Come in. Scrivens was telling me that you've been to Wombwell.'

'Yes, sir. Saw the old lady. Peel fitted a stairlift for her today. Left there about a quarter past five.'

'Did he seem…all right?'

'She didn't think there was anything peculiar about him?'

'Where was he going? Did she know?'

'Thought he said he was going home.'

'What time does the shop close?'

'Five thirty, sir,' Carter said. 'They weren't expecting him back tonight. Anyway, he wouldn't have reached it before it closed. The man at the shop gave me Angus Peel's home address, landline and mobile number. He said he'd phone me if he turned up before they closed. There's no reply from his mobile or his house phone. I've tried it a few times.'

Angel rubbed his chin. He didn't like it. 'You've been to his house?' he asked.

'It's deserted, sir. I was there about an hour ago. Looked all round it. Nobody answered the doorbell.'

It was this last suspect that worried Angel. 'I'll have a look,' he said. 'He's the last one. I can't leave it like this. He might be the one. Then I'm going home.'

'I'll show you where it is, sir,' Carter said. 'It'll save time.'

Angel nodded.

Ahmed said, 'A patrol car's picking me up at the front now, sir.'

'Right, lad. Now be careful.'

Ahmed dashed out of the office.

Angel turned to Scrivens. 'DS Crisp is bringing in a woman called Margaret Ireland. She'll be processed and formally admitted into protection. Tell the desk sergeant that I've arranged for a place for her at the safe house on Beechfield Walk. She is to be searched and her belongings searched. And she is to be carefully observed. There needs to be two officers in attendance with her, never one only. But I don't want her to think that we suspect her, but, of course, we do. Just tell her that it's the system and that we're just being careful.'

Scrivens nodded. 'Right, sir.'

'You can also tell him that DS Carter is with me and we are going down to Angus Peel's house to see if we can raise him. Then, if I'm not back, help Ahmed process and settle Kenneth Lamb into a cell and push off home. All right?'

'Right, sir,' he said, he went out and closed the door.

Angel turned back to Carter and said, 'You've instructed the duty jailer, the cells of the men are not to be unlocked at the same time?'

'Yes, sir.'

'They're not to think they're prisoners, but I can't risk one murdering the other.'

'He understands that, sir,' she said.

'Right. Let's go.'

Five minutes later, at nine o'clock exactly, two cars arrived at the front of the small, modern bungalow on the Wothersley estate, Carter in her Ford followed by Angel in his BMW. Daylight was fading quickly. It was still light enough to see the road, but it was necessary to use sidelights. They parked their cars and met up at the front gate.

Angel saw that there were no lights on in the bungalow. He stepped up to the front door. Carter followed. There was an air of neglect about the place. While the doorknob and the keyhole were well used, the white paintwork on the door needed a good clean down and small cobwebs removed from across the corners of the lintel. There was a bell push at the side. He pressed it and heard chimes ring out inside.

They waited. There was no reply. They looked at each other.

'Just like it was before, sir,' Carter said.

He nodded. 'Have a walk round, sergeant. See if all the window glass is sound and the back door is locked.'

She rushed off.

Angel pressed the bell again.

Then suddenly he heard a voice, a loud, raucous voice, a voice that sounded as if the owner of it gargled with formaldehyde. 'Hey, you there.'

Angel looked round.

The bellowing came from a big man in a vest and jeans standing outside the open door of the bungalow next door.

'Who are *you*?' he bawled. '*What* are you? Jehovah's Witnesses? He's out. I saw your mate earlier. You never give up, do you? Pity you haven't got homes to go to.'

Angel called back, 'I'm a police officer. I want to speak to Mr Angus Peel on a very urgent matter. Who are you, sir?'

The tone of the man changed. 'Oh? Police?' he said, and he came across his drive to the low concrete and wire fence between the two bungalows.

Angel crossed to meet him. He waved his warrant card in his direction, even though it was too dark for the man to be able to read it.

'He's out,' the man said. 'His van isn't here. We're trying to keep the estate respectable, you know? There's always somebody knocking on our doors trying to peddle us something. Not always honest.'

Angel knew what he meant. 'Any idea where Mr Peel might be?'

'He works late hours occasionally and sometimes eats out or brings in a takeaway. Don't know what he gets up to,' he said. 'I think he's got a bird on the side,' he added with a snigger.

Angel's eyebrows went up. 'Any idea of her name or address?'

'No. It was only a joke.'

'You said something about someone calling earlier.'

'Yes. Strange looking chap. I thought *he* was a Jehovah's Witness.'

'Can you describe him? It might be important.'

'Easy. He was dressed in a white cloak thing, like...like Lawrence of Arabia. He had a beard. I saw him through the front window. He was knocking on Angus's door. Strange. He'd gone by the time I got outside to see what he wanted.'

Angel's heart began to beat like a tom-tom.

Carter arrived back from checking the windows. She saw Angel conversing with the man and rushed up to join them. Angel lifted his head and looked at her.

'Nothing, sir,' she said.

Angel turned back to the man. 'Anything else?' he said.

'Don't know,' the man said. 'I said I only caught a glimpse. He had a lot of hair, black or dark brown. Can't think. He looked like the figures you see in big, old churches.'

Angel's mind was in turmoil. He must keep calm. 'What time was this?'

'Oh, I don't know....'

Angel eyed the man closely. He looked yellow in the glow of the halogen streetlight. 'Could be very important,' he said. 'Very important indeed.'

The man frowned. 'Between five and six,' he said. 'No, it was six o'clock exactly. I remember now. I was watching the telly and the news had just started.'

Angel rubbed his chin.

Carter said, 'How tall was he?'

'About your height,' he said.

'Five feet, eight inches?' she said. 'Did he come in a car?'

'Don't know. Didn't see one.'

'When he left, which way did he go?'

'Don't know. That's all I can tell you.'

Angel said, 'What's Mr Peel's van like?'

'It's a white Ford Transit van, new. He's only had it a few weeks.'

'Right,' Angel said. 'Thanks very much. If he turns up, tell him that...tell him we want him to report to the police station very urgently.'

'Yes, all right. Is he in trouble?'

Angel didn't want to ring any alarm bells. 'No. Nothing like that.'

'The other chap, the chap dressed like an Arab...are you looking for him? Is he a villain?'

Carter looked at Angel who said, 'Something like that.'

'If he comes back, I'll give you a bell,' the man said.

Angel reckoned the man couldn't tell them any more. 'Thank you very much,' he said. 'Good night.'

When he was out of earshot, he turned to Carter and said, 'I don't like this. I don't like this one bit. I'm going to put this place under observation in case Peel or the murderer turn up. And I'll get Traffic to transmit a notice to stop all new white Ford Transits they see in the district.'

'Anything I can do, sir?'

'Yes. Go home and get some sleep. You'll need to be on top form tomorrow.'

CHAPTER NINE

It was after ten o'clock when Angel arrived home.

Mary was furious.

'I phoned the station twice,' she said. 'Nobody knew where *you* were, and there was nobody there *I* knew well enough to ask where you were. Even Superintendent Harker had gone home.'

'I'm sorry, Mary. You know what it's like when there's a murder on.'

'Surely you've time to phone.'

'I suppose...but I forget. It gets so busy, so intense.'

'You soon remember to come home when...when you're hungry.'

'I'm not hungry. Couldn't face a thing.'

Mary's eyes flashed. 'There's a fine thing to say. That was best English lamb. It's ruined now, Michael. I couldn't possibly reheat it. You'll have to have it cold, tomorrow with salad.

'I'm sorry, love,' he said. 'You have to understand -'

'But I don't understand,' she said as she stormed out to the kitchen. 'Honestly, I don't know why I bother,' she said, slamming the door and making the lampshades on the chandelier rattle.

Then followed a clattering racket from pots and pans and cutlery being banged about, making more noise than a New Years' Day riot in the cookhouse at Strangeways.

He leaned back in the chair and closed his eyes. Highlights of the day's events kept coming back at him. He sat in silence. Time passed by. He wasn't certain how long. The noise from the kitchen had subsided. The door quietly opened and Mary came in. He didn't seem to notice.

She looked at him for a few moments, then sat on the arm of his chair, leaned over and kissed him on the forehead.

He looked back at her, nodded, put his hand on hers and squeezed it.

'What would you like?' she said. 'I've got some eggs, and -'

'No. Honestly. A cup of tea's fine. That's all I want.'

She hesitated, then patted his hand again, glanced at the television, reached over to the remote control, pressed the button to switch it on then stood up and returned to the kitchen.

He watched her go and smiled. He settled back in the chair.

The volume on the TV came up. It was loud, dramatic music, but his eyelids closed and he fell asleep.

*

The alarm clock rang.

Angel reached out of bed and cancelled it. It was 7.30, Friday morning.

Mary edged up the bed, whisked back the duvet and dangled her legs over the side, fishing around for her slippers.

Angel reached out for the phone and tapped in a number.

Mary turned round and stared at him. 'Who on earth are you disturbing at this time in a morning?'

'Checking up to see if the lads outside Angus Peel's house have turned anything up.'

'Poor souls. It is only 7.30. Why don't you give them another hour or so?'

He was soon speaking to one of the two men skulking in a car parked at the opposite side of the road two car lengths from Peel's bungalow. The conversation was short and negative. He banged down the receiver.

'Nothing,' he said.

Mary was in the bathroom. She didn't hear.

He grunted then reached out for the phone again.

He tapped in the number of the Control Room.

'Did you get any reports about white Ford Transits overnight, Sergeant?'

'Yes, sir. Let me see...here we are. Three were seen and stopped, sir. None belonged to that disabled supplies shop. All index numbers were checked and all were engaged in legal business.'

'Thank you, Sergeant,' he said. 'I hope you had a quiet night?'

'Two drunks fighting outside The Feathers, a domestic on Canal Road, that's all, sir.'

'Right. Thank you.' He frowned as he slowly replaced the phone.

'Bathroom's free,' Mary called.

'Coming,' he said and whisked back the duvet.

'I don't know why you don't get a proper job like teaching,' Mary said. 'With nice, respectable people, where you keep normal hours and you don't have to work all hours, and phone people at all hours. And I would know for certain you'd be home at 5.30, without a knife in your back or a bullet in your chest.'

'Don't be so melodramatic,' he said. 'I've never had a serious injury yet, nor ever likely to have.'

There were several more similar exchanges over the breakfast table. He'd heard them all before.

Mary gave him an extra-long kiss before he left for the office that morning. It was by way of apology for complaining so much. He was fully aware of it. He knew all her moods. He adored her and there was nothing he wouldn't do for her, except give up being a policeman. He liked being a copper. And he liked being DI Angel, the policeman who *always* unravels the mystery and gets the murderer. And *she* was aware of *that*. She just had to let off a bit of steam sometimes when it took him away from her and she thought he might be putting himself in danger.

*

It was 08.28 hours when he walked into the office. Ahmed saw him arrive from his desk in CID and followed him in. 'Good morning, sir.'

'Good morning, lad. Did you settle Mr Lamb in all right?'

'He was a lot of trouble, sir. Objected to being put in a cell. Wanted to return home.'

'But you've got him locked up, haven't you?'

'Yes, sir. He was demanding to see the Chief Constable.'

Angel grunted, then said, 'He'll have to put up with me. But we need to find Angus Peel first. Phone that shop where he works. See if he's turned up for work. You never know. I don't know what else we can do.'

Ahmed was about to pick up the phone when it rang. He answered it. 'Inspector Angel's office.'

'Control Room. Is the inspector there?'

Ahmed held the phone out. 'It's the Control Room, sir.'

Angel took the phone, 'Angel speaking.'

'About that Ford Transit van, sir. It's turned up. A man fishing in the canal on Canal Road noticed the roof of a white vehicle just under the water. I sent a patrol car there. From the other side of the canal, the patrolman could see the index plate. And that's the one.'

Angel's heart began pounding. 'Thank you, Sergeant. Any idea how it got there?'

'He said it had mounted a low wall, sir, so it looks to have been deliberately driven in there at speed. It's going to have to be lifted out. It'll need a heavy crane.'

'SOCO will see to that. Instruct the patrolman to stay there until some uniformed arrive, will you? I wouldn't want nosey swimmers or anybody else interfering with it.'

'Right, sir.'

He replaced the phone and breathed out a long sigh. If Peel was dead in the van, then one of the two men in the cells or the woman in the safe house had to be the murderer. If he wasn't, then he has still to be found and it won't be a moment too soon, because he could very well be the murderer on the loose.

He turned to Ahmed. 'Go to your own phone and ring DS Maroney, of Leeds Police Underwater Team. Give him my compliments. Tell him we've a job for him and his team, and ask him to come over ASAP.'

'Right, sir,' he said and he went out.

Angel picked up the phone and tapped in a number.

'SOLO,' Taylor said.

'We might have found the whereabouts of Angus Peel, Don,' Angel said.

*

Angel went down to Canal Road and had a quick look at the scene then quickly returned to his office.

He phoned Don Taylor to instruct him to organize the hoisting of the van out of the canal ASAP, and to liaise with DS Maroney of the Leeds Police Underwater Team.

He had just replaced the phone when there was a knock at the door.

'Come in.'

It was Ahmed.

'What is it, lad.'

'There's a message from the duty jailer, sir. It's that Lamb in cell four. He's kicking up and wants to see you.'

'Yes. I expect he does. Tell him I haven't forgotten him. I'll see him soon.'

The phone rang.

Angel reached out for it and at the same time waved Ahmed to carry on.

Ahmed went out and closed the door.

It was WPC Baverstock. 'Margaret Ireland here at the safe house wants to see you, sir. She's rather fed up with being here.'

Angel sighed. 'Yes. All right, Leisha. Ask her to be patient and tell her I will definitely see her today.'

'Right, sir.'

He replaced the phone. It rang out again. He picked it up.

'Angel,' he said.

It was Harker. 'Come up here,' he growled, then there was a loud click as he slammed the phone down.

Angel pulled a face. It could only be trouble. When Harker wanted to see him it was always trouble. He replaced the phone, trudged up the green corridor to the superintendent's office, tapped on the door and went in.

The skinny man with the big ginger eyebrows had a white plastic inhaler up a nostril. He looked at Angel out of the side of his eyes.

'Come in,' he said, pulling the inhaler down and shoving it up the other nostril. After a long sniff, he withdrew it, replaced the cap and dropped it in the pocket of the cheap, ill-fitting navy-blue suit coat. His father-in-law had died recently and Angel thought he must have inherited the suit from him.

Angel closed the door and went up to his desk.

'What the bloody hell's going on?' Harker said. 'I passed the cells and found two men in there. I asked the jailer what's going on and he said that they were there under your instructions. I asked him what they were charged with and he said that they weren't charged, they were there for their own protection. I said against *what*, and he said he didn't know. Next, I arrived here in my office to find an indent from WPC Baverstock for meals for a woman in the safe house. I got hold of Baverstock on the phone and I asked her who or what is the woman being protected against and she said one of the two men in cells. I said which one. She said she didn't know. I thought as they are both locked up what on earth has she to be protected against? What sort of a police station are we operating here? It seems to me it's a freebie hotel for scroungers. What on earth is happening?'

Angel sighed. He knew Harker would make it difficult if he found out what was happening. 'It's simple enough, sir. One of the three is a murderer, committed to murdering the other two, but I don't know which one.'

'Eh? I see. It's a new procedure, is it? Put all the suspects in cells, and we are certain to include the guilty one. Huh. I'm not sure we will have enough cells, but I am certain that the CPS wouldn't be able to construct a case against all three at the same time, should you take them to court.' He shook his head. 'I don't know. I don't understand. You're supposed to be the whiz-kid detective that always gets his man, the tabloid paper's darling. Frankly, Angel, I think you've finally gone off your chump.'

Angel explained about the messages in blood daubed on the mirrors and then went on to inform him that there was a fourth missing suspect/victim and that his van was at that time being retrieved from the canal.

Harker's bloodshot eyes flashed. 'You've brought in a crane?'

'There is no other way, sir.'

'That'll be over three thousand pounds,' he bawled. 'This case is getting well out of hand. Is the man's body in the van?'

'Don't know that yet, sir.'

'*You don't know*?' he bawled. 'Yet you've set engineers on to bring it up? You're floundering around, Angel, aren't you? And you're doing everything the most expensive way. You could have sent a diver down to see. If a body isn't there, you could leave the van in the water. The insurance company might have brought it up, at *their* expense.'

Angel clenched his fists. 'Yes, sir, but if there's any forensic, I need it now, to prevent more murders. Also, the insurance company may never have lifted it. We can't wait. I need to preserve every scrap of evidence there might be. He's killed two we know about and has threatened to kill another four. He means business. We are fortunate in this case, as I happen to have found out who his prospective victims are.'

'And the murderer, according to you, is one of them, meanwhile they are enjoying three-star accommodation at the expense of the force.'

'I am awaiting a DNA report from Wetherby on hairs found on the body of Luke Redman. I am expecting it to prove which one of the suspects is the murderer.'

'When do you expect it?'

'Monday next.'

'I think that's about as long as I can afford to support this three-ring circus. You've got until Monday, then, to sort something out. I will not sanction any more payment for meals for residents in this police station who are not charged with some offence after Monday. All right?'

It wasn't all right, but what could Angel do?

He came out of Harker's office and marched down to his own office. He went in and banged the door. Everything seemed to rest upon the DNA of those two hairs found on Redman. He had not taken samples of the DNA from the three suspects for comparison to avoid arousing their suspicions. If they had been asked for swabs, they would surely have become wary. However, there was another aspect of the DNA result that had just come to him. The owner of the two hairs might be on the police national database, and it takes only minutes to get a response from that.

*

'Mr Lamb,' Angel said. 'I thought we'd talk in this interview room, informally; there's no recording being made. Sorry to keep you waiting.'

'I should think so. I've been kept in that cell all night, locked up, like a common criminal.'

Angel pointed to a chair and then pursed his lips. He wanted to put this man completely at ease, but it was difficult. It wasn't easy for him to pretend to be convivial to anybody he knew might be a murderer.

'It's for your own safety, sir. You're not a prisoner, you know. By the way, this is Detective Sergeant Carter. Police Constable Ahaz you've met.'

Lamb nodded at her across the table. She nodded back. He ignored Ahmed.

'I feel like a prisoner. Who am I being protected against anyway?'

'The murderer of Luke Redman and Ingrid Underwood.'

'Yes,' he said quickly, 'but who is he, what's his name?'

'We're not sure about that, Mr Lamb. We know that it is one of the survivors of that production of *Nero* twenty years ago at the Variety Theatre. I hoped you might be able to help us there.'

Lamb's mouth dropped open. 'There can't be many survivors. A lot of the members were quite old when we tried to stage it then.'

'Which one of them would have a motive?'

'Young Malcolm Malloy,' Lamb said promptly. 'But he died. That fire ruined his life. He was a promising actor. We were very lucky - or we thought we were - to get him in the players to play the lead. He had trained at RADA and everybody thought he promised to be the next Kenneth Branagh.'

Angel nodded. 'Where did he live?'

'Don't know.'

'What about his family? Was he married?'

'No, but I remember the girls were all over him at rehearsals. He was in great demand.'

Angel passed his hand through his hair. He didn't seem to be getting anywhere.

Lamb said, 'What makes you think that the murderer wants to murder *me*?'

'I'm not at liberty to tell you that, Mr Lamb, just now. Trust me. I have your best interests at heart.'

The man frowned. He wasn't pleased. 'Whatever do you mean?' he said.

Angel looked into his eyes.

'Well,' Lamb began, 'who are the others still living? I expect I shall remember them.'

Angel blew out a small, non-existent candle and said, 'There's Angus Peel, Tom Franks and Margaret Ireland. Would any of those have a motive for wanting you dead?'

Angel noticed the man's fingers shake very slightly.

Lamb licked his lips and said, 'I don't know, do I?'

There were a few more fruitless exchanges between the two men before Lamb was shown back to his cell and Angel returned to his office.

Angel's phone was ringing as he reached the door. He reached over the desk and snatched it up.

It was Taylor. 'Yes, Don?'

'The crane people are worried about the safety of the canal bank, sir. They don't want their crane sliding or tipping into the water. So the canal bank is going to have to be strengthened with a platform of steel girders. They are also sending for a special crane, which is in a yard in Wolverhampton and is being loaded on to a low-loader as we speak. This will all take time. Looks like thirty-six hours at least.'

Angel wasn't pleased. 'The longer they take the colder the crime scene.'

'Nothing we can do about it, sir,' Taylor said.

'Right, lad,' he said and rang off.

CHAPTER TEN

DC Scrivens and WPC Baverstock brought Margaret Ireland from the safe house into Interview Room number 1. She was a tall, lean woman who looked as if she spent all day on exercise machines and only ate chicken and lettuce. In the presence of DS Carter and PC Ahaz, Angel went through an exchange of information with her. Her questions and answers were almost the same as Lamb's. However, in reply to a question about Malcolm Malloy, she became most animated and said, 'His stage presence was quite magnetic, Inspector. You knew when he was there even if he hadn't any lines to say. Also, he was the most handsome man you could ever want to meet. He appealed to women of every age. You couldn't help but fall for him.'

'Was there any significant woman in his life?'

She smiled for a moment as she remembered. 'He seemed pointedly not to get too close to anyone. He was hell bent on being a successful actor...nothing else mattered to him.'

'You knew him well?'

'Oh yes. He played Nero, you know, and I played a young girl, Aristana, who seduced him. He was a thoroughly vile character, who treated her very badly and eventually murdered her in a most revolting way at the end of Act 2, so we spent a lot of time together at rehearsals.'

'Do you know where he lived?'

'Somewhere on Huddersfield Road, I think.'

'What about his parents, his family?'

'I'm sorry, I have no idea.'

Angel rubbed his chin.

'Look here, Inspector,' she said. 'How much longer will I have to stay in police protection?'

'Until Monday, I should think,' he said. 'I am awaiting some forensic evidence, Miss Ireland, that should confirm the identity of the murderer. It will be here on Monday.'

'You have a suspect?'

Angel nodded. 'And it's someone directly concerned with that play,' he said slyly.

With raised eyebrows, she said, 'Most of them will have passed on. But I am not the only survivor.'

'No,' Angel said, wondering how he was going to head off the next question. But he couldn't.

'Who else is still alive?'

He wrinkled his nose. 'Angus Peel, Tom Franks and Kenneth Lamb.'

The blood drained from her face when she heard the names.

*

As Angel drove his BMW down Wakefield Road and turned into Canal Road, he came among a crowd of vehicles parked on the grass verge close to the place where the white van was submerged. There were two police cars, the SOCO van, two Range Rovers with signs on their doors that read 'Leeds Police Underwater Team', a lorry loaded with steel girders and at least three other cars. He supposed that the cars belonged to the outside building team that had to be brought in by the SOCO.

He spotted a suitable place to leave the BMW, turned off the road and parked it on the grass verge behind the SOCO van.

There were four men Angel didn't know. They were wearing high-visibility waistcoats and hard hats, and holding measuring tapes stretched across the canal. Also there were two uniformed policemen leaning over the bridge wall watching events, and DS Taylor of SOCO standing at the edge of the water, talking to two men in black diving suits.

Taylor and the divers broke away when they saw Angel striding over a low, damaged stone wall and making his way up the slope to the bank.

'Have you been down yet,' Angel said as he reached them.

'Just going, sir,' DS Maroney said.

Taylor said, 'Been waiting for you, sir.'

'You shouldn't have bothered,' Angel replied and turned to the other young man in the diving suit. 'Who is this then?'

'DC Cutts, sir,' Maroney said. 'Colin, this is Inspector Angel.'

Cutts smiled. 'Pleased to meet you, sir. Heard a lot about you.'

Angel thought it sounded like a compliment. He was momentarily at a loss for words. 'Oh? Right, lad,' he said after a pause. 'Er...good. Well, carry on, in your own time. This is DS Taylor's show.'

Maroney looked at Taylor who nodded and smiled. He then turned to Cutts and said, 'Right, Colin.'

The two divers put on their flippers, adjusted clips on their noses, turned on their oxygen bottles, inserted the mouthpieces, jumped into the water and paddled and then swam across to the submerged van.

As they disappeared from sight, Angel turned to Taylor and said, 'What exactly have you told them to do?'

'To see if there's a body there, sir. That's all we can do, until the van is lifted out of the water.'

Angel wrinkled his nose. 'If there is a body down there, I need to know whose it is.'

'It might not be possible without disturbing possible forensic, sir.'

It was true. But Angel wondered just how much forensic evidence of value in this particular case was likely to survive, being submerged for two days or so in that dirty water. He also thought that the defence barrister would have an easy time discrediting almost any DNA that might have been found in such a contaminated environment, that that principle in these circumstances was valueless.

He walked round to the bridge past the two constables and leaned over the wall so as to be as near the divers as possible when they surfaced. Taylor followed and stood next to him. Then the two men looked down at the roof of the van still visible under a foot or so of dirty water and tried to see the divers. The water had become muddy and all they managed to make out were a few bubbles and the flash of a flipper from time to time. Suddenly, Cutts's head came out of the water followed by Maroney's. The two men were treading water. Maroney looked round, found Angel, took out the mouthpiece and said, 'There is the body of a man in the co-driver's seat, sir.'

'Can you describe him,' Angel said.

Maroney removed the nose clip and shook his head. 'No sir. Only to say he has a good head of hair.'

'Can you open the van door?' Angel said.

Taylor wasn't pleased. 'There's the possibility of prints on it, sir,' he said.

'I *know*,' Angel said then he turned back to Maroney. 'Disturbing as little as possible, could you open the door, pull back the dead man's head and take a photograph?'

Taylor looked away.

Maroney spat out water running down his cheeks into his mouth. 'Yes, sir,' he said.

Cutts said, 'Shall I see if I can open the door first, sir?' Angel said, 'Be very careful, lad. Do not touch anything inside. Just see if the door will open.'

'Right, sir,' Cutts said, and inserting the mouthpiece, he plunged under the water, briefly showed a flipper and then disappeared.

Out of his eye corner, Angel saw Taylor shaking his head as he walked down the bridge away from him.

Maroney, still treading water, sensed there was something wrong and said, 'Is there a problem, sir?'

Angel promptly said, 'No.'

Taylor turned round, came back up to Angel and said 'With respect, sir. The van is a crime scene and should be sealed off until it is out of the water.'

Angel sighed, looked back at Maroney and said, 'Hold it a minute.' Then he glared at Taylor and said, 'I know all about procedure and crime scenes, Don. I've been spoon-fed with them for years. I had them with my Virol. But I need to know whose body it is down there and how he died, and I simply can't wait forty-eight hours. It may be that of a victim or of the murderer. There are people up here who are very much alive and I am doing my damnedest to keep them like that, while, at the same time, one of them is doing his damnedest to murder the rest. And I don't know which is which. Now they are safe at the moment, but the Super insists that I withdraw that guarantee in forty-eight hours. Now, I haven't the luxury of having time to possibly - only possibly - wait for you to find a giveaway hair or spec of skin in that filthy water that *might* make a case against one of them that would stick in court. While we are abiding by the rules, somebody else may be getting murdered. So don't let's waste any more time.'

Taylor shrugged and said, 'Right, sir. You're the boss.'

Angel turned back to Maroney.

'We have a camera, heavy duty batteries and underwater light source in the 4 x 4,' Maroney said.

Cutts's head bobbed up out of the water. He removed the oxygen pipe and the nose clip. 'I've managed to open the van door, sir,' he said brightly.

Maroney said, 'Right, sir. What exactly do you want us to do, sir?'

Angel said, 'I want a photograph of the face of the character in the van in situ. And I want you to see if there is a wound in the chest. And if there is, the approximate position of it. Can you do that?'

'I think so, sir. We can give it a try,' Maroney said.

'Disturbing as little as you can?' Taylor said.

'Of course,' Maroney said.

Angel then turned back to Taylor, patted him on the back and said, 'I leave it to you, Don. Let me know how you get on.

'Right, sir,' Taylor said.

Then Angel climbed down the bank to his car and returned to the station.

He had been in his office, writing up his report about an hour when there was a knock at the door. It was DS Taylor. He hurried in with a wet 7" x 5" photograph in his hand.

'Will you have a look at this, sir?'

Angel took it and was taken aback. It wasn't pleasant. The dark photograph, brown almost sepia, showed a distorted face with a huge nose and tiny ears. The features were reproduced adequately, with the eyes closed and the hair flowing as if it was growing out of the head like snakes.

'Because the water was so mucky, Maroney had to stick the camera so close to his face, it has made the photograph distorted,' Taylor said.

'I can see that, Don, but do you think *anyone* could identify anybody with certainty from that?'

Taylor rubbed his chin.

'It's nearly as obscene as my passport photograph,' Angel said.

Taylor hesitated then said, 'Shall I go back and see if Maroney can find a still moment maybe...for the water to clear and try again?'

'*Anything*,' Angel said, passing his hand through his hair impatiently. He pushed the photograph into Taylor's hand then added, 'But let's get this chap identified.'

Taylor rushed out.

It was two hours later when he returned.

'I can confirm that the dead man is Angus Peel, sir. DS Maroney managed to get a better photograph of the victim's head, and I took it to the manager of the shop where he worked and to his next door neighbour and they both agreed it was him.'

Angel blew out a truncheon's length of breath.

'Also, Maroney cut open the dead man's shirt front,' Taylor said, 'and found an open wound near the solar plexus.'

Angel sighed and pursed his lips.

'So we have one more body and one less suspect. We now know the murderer is Tom Franks, Margaret Ireland or Kenneth Lamb. How on earth are we to establish which one? For an alibi, I need to know the time of death. If I asked Mac that, I can just imagine what he would reply...about a body that's been in water an indeterminate length of time.'

Taylor smiled.

Angel suddenly went quiet. His eyes narrowed. He said, 'It's possible that I could work out the time of death.'

'How's that, sir?' Taylor said.

'Carter was told by a customer in Mexborough the time that he had left her, having installed a stairlift that day. It was late afternoon sometime, but she had it exactly.'

'Yes, sir,' Taylor said.

'And Peel could not have been murdered after the last suspect of the three suspects, Franks, Ireland and Lamb, had been warned and brought here. It had to be...late afternoon, early evening.'

Taylor's face brightened. 'That's right, sir.'

Angel reached out for the phone. 'Ahmed,' he said into the mouthpiece. 'Find DS Carter. And DS Crisp. I want them here, smartly.' He replaced the phone, turned to Taylor and said, 'You'd better get back to Canal Road, Don.'

'Right, sir,' Taylor said and he dashed off.

Carter was the first to arrive in Angel's office. Ahmed came in with her.

'DS Crisp is on the way, sir.'

Angel's eyes were bright and searching. He looked closely at Carter and said, 'What time did the woman in Mexborough, who had had her stairlift fitted, say that Angus Peel left her house?'

'Five fifteen that afternoon, sir,' Carter said.

Angel nodded. 'So that's the last time he was seen alive, wasn't it?'

'To my knowledge, sir, yes.'

'So 5.16 on Thursday was the earliest that Angus Peel could have been murdered.'

He turned to Ahmed. 'And what time did you first make contact with Kenneth Lamb?'

'That was on the phone, sir. That was about 8.30 that evening.'

Angel glared up at him. 'Can't you do any better than that, lad? *About*? Can't you be more accurate?'

Ahmed whipped out his notebook and shuffled back through a couple of pages. 'Sorry, sir. Yes. It was *exactly* 8.30, sir.'

Angel nodded. 'Right. Now Lamb was the last...er... candidate to be brought in, so...stabbing Peel and getting the van in the canal would have taken at least 30 minutes. I estimate that if Lamb is the murderer, Peel would have been murdered by him sometime between 5.16 and 8 o'clock, at a stretch.'

Carter nodded.

'Making the same sort of calculation re Margaret Ireland,' Angel said, 'Peel would have been murdered by her between 5.16 and 8.10, and Franks, between 5.16 and...if my memory serves me right...6.30.'

'So Lamb had a bigger window of time to commit the murder and drive the van into the canal,' Carter said.

'You could say that, yes.'

'Can't see a woman wielding a dagger and dumping the van in a canal, like that, sir,' Ahmed said.

'True,' Angel said. 'But we must keep all options open. Women have been known to commit crimes even more odious and requiring much more mechanical expertise than driving a van into a canal.'

'Mr Franks is much more of a gentleman than Mr Lamb, sir,' Ahmed said. 'But, I know, we can't let external impressions affect our judgement either.'

Angel nodded, then he said, 'We now have to see what alibis they have.'

There was a knock at the door. It was Crisp.

Angel glared at him.

Crisp's eyes were shining. 'I've got something that you will be very interested in, sir. You know I was called in by a shop on Market Street that was having white bed sheets lifted repeatedly.'

'Yes, lad?' Angel said.

'The shop has tables outside on the pavement with all kinds of textiles piled up on them, sir. They were stolen from there.'

Angel's face suddenly changed. 'White sheets, lad? Did you say *white* bed sheets stolen?'

'There's CCTV, sir. From inside the shop. I've been going through it in the theatre. I am sure I recognize the thief.'

The team bounded down to the theatre and crowded round the 30" screen as Crisp ran the tape. At the bottom right-hand corner of the picture was the time and date: 13.01. 28.05.09.

The CCTV camera was positioned inside the shop looking outside through the window at several tables piled high with towels, tea towels, pillow cases and sheets in white and all colours and sizes. Each pile had a cardboard price ticket stuck on the top. The pile of white sheets were at the end, wrapped in cellophane and tied with a broad band of red ribbon. Crowds of people passed by on the pavement without even glancing at the merchandise, but occasionally a shopper, usually a woman or two women together, stopped, looked at the stock, read the price tag, dallied a while then moved out of the picture. Whether they sallied into the shop and bought some or simply ambled along the pavement was not clear. However, unusually, the figure of a tall man in a large overcoat and trilby hat suddenly appeared out of the crowd. He shuffled by the table, quickly reached out, deftly pulled two packs of white sheets from the pile on the table, tucked them under his overcoat and was gone. Although he had been surrounded by people, nobody in the crowd seemed to notice what had happened.

In the theatre, with one voice, the team said, 'It's Lamb!'

'Run it back, Trevor,' Angel said. 'Run it again.'

Crisp ran the tape back and then replayed it. At the point where the man's face was the most exposed, Angel said, 'Stop the tape.'

Crisp pressed the button.

Everybody stared at the screen. They all agreed it was Lamb.

Angel shook his head. '*Looks* like Lamb,' he said. 'But he doesn't look to see if he's being seen by anybody. He doesn't even check to see if there's any CCTV. He doesn't attempt to hide his face with a handkerchief as if he was wiping his nose, or lower his head to avoid being seen. There's something wrong.'

Crisp frowned and looked at Carter and then at Ahmed.

They all stared at the screen again.

'I do believe it's Lamb, sir,' Crisp said.

Carter said, 'Or his twin brother.'

Ahmed nodded.

Angel said nothing.

'Shall I interview him, sir?' Crisp said. 'See what he has to say about it?'

Angel blinked a few times then said: 'All right. Why not? You can ask him about taking the sheets. See how far you get. Then you can see what sort of an alibi he puts up for the time from 5.16 and 8 o'clock last night. Record the interview. Do it to the letter. You'll have to find him a solicitor. Get Bloomfield unless he has one of his own. Ahmed can sit in with you. It'll be good experience.'

Ahmed smiled.

'Crack on then, lad. Don't mess about.'

'Right, sir,' Crisp said and he dashed out of the theatre. Ahmed hovered. He wasn't certain whether he should stay there with Angel or go now with Crisp.

Angel saw the hesitation. 'Go on, Ahmed,' he said. 'Stick with him.'

'Right, sir,' he said and dashed off.

Angel turned to Carter. 'I want you to go to Dr Suliman and get a warrant to search Lamb's house. The duty sergeant will give you his address. In particular, look for these stolen bedsheets, of course, and a trilby hat and an overcoat to match these on the tape, but much more importantly a silver dagger, a laurel bush and a pair of sandals. Also look in his garden. See if the ground has been turned over recently...if any bloodstained sheets have been buried. Take Ted Scrivens with you.'

'Right, sir,' she said, her eyes shining, and made for the door. Then she stopped, turned back and said, 'How do you know it's a *silver* dagger, sir?'

'Ask me again when time isn't at such a premium. Now *shoo*!' he said and out she ran.

Angel was in the theatre alone. He promptly moved to the seat in front of the console. He ran the tape back, then played it on slow. He peered closely at the screen as the pictures clicked slowly past. Several times he stopped the movement of the tape and peered at the picture. When he had run it to the end of the piece, he rewound it and ran it back again. He did this for more than an hour, when Inspector Asquith from uniformed division came into the theatre wanting to use the screen. Angel was surprised to see that the time was 5.45 p.m.

CHAPTER ELEVEN

The week end. Eight o'clock on Saturday morning, 30 May. Angel was still in bed, wide awake, looking at the ceiling. Summer had arrived. The sun was shining, the birds were coughing, the Rottweilers barking, thieves were stealing, prisoners were planning to escape.

Mary appeared round the door. He heard the rustle of her housecoat and turned to look at her. She was more beautiful than a bower of fresh flowers.

'The shower's free, darling,' she said.

'Right,' he said.

She went out.

'Breakfast in ten minutes,' she said as she glided along the hall.

'Aye,' he said, without commitment, as he swivelled round to the edge of the bed and dropped his feet into his slippers.

The weekend...well, *this* weekend anyway, was a...a disruption.

He wrinkled his nose, sniffed, stared briefly at the white anaglypta, stretched out his arms and ran a hand through his hair.

This break from work served no useful purpose whatsoever. It was an unnecessary and annoying disruption to his search for the serial killer. There were all sorts of inquiries he should be making. He wanted to listen to some of those recorded interviews again. He wanted to get his mind clear for Monday morning. Harker wanted those cells empty by then. God knows he didn't want to let a murderer go free but that seems what he might have to do.

He had been considering whether he might risk suggesting to Mary that he might go into the office. She got very ratty if he suggested that he went in when he was off duty. He couldn't quite understand her. It wasn't that she wanted him for any particular reason. He reckoned that it was simply that she didn't want it to seem that he preferred his work to her, which wasn't the case nor ever could be. Mary was the moon with jam on it, and he didn't want to hurt her. Nevertheless, it would be great if the duty sergeant phoned to say that some emergency had cropped up to give him the excuse he wanted.

He looked at the phone at the side of the bed, but it didn't ring, nor would it.

He ambled to the bathroom, rinsed his face in cold water and cleaned his teeth.

Over breakfast, Mary said, 'Are you cutting the lawn this morning, Michael? It needs it.'

'Oh? I hadn't noticed,' he lied.

'Ideal conditions. Nice and dry. And the borders need weeding.'

'Oh? Yes, love.'

'The hedge needs trimming too.'

Angel sighed. He knew that Mary had skilfully hijacked his weekend.

*

When Angel went out of the front door of his bungalow on the morning of Monday, 1 June he felt like a rat that had been let out of a trap.

He reached his office at 8.20 and immediately reached for the phone to summon Ahmed. While it was ringing out, there was a knock at the door.

'Come in.'

It was Ahmed.

Angel banged down the phone. 'I was trying to reach you, lad.'

'I was in reception, sir,' Ahmed said. 'There's a woman, Rosemary Underwood, wants to see the person in charge of the investigation into her mother's murder.'

Angel wrinkled his nose. 'Oh yes. Mrs Underwood's daughter, next of kin. It's about time she showed up. Poor lass. She might be able to throw some light on things. Have you made her comfortable?'

'Put her in the front interview room, sir. She didn't want a cup of tea or anything.'

'Good. I'll see to her. She'll have to wait a bit. She's picked a busy day.'

Ahmed pulled a curious face and then said, 'There's something I'd like to say, sir.'

Angel looked up at him. It was an unusual comment for Ahmed to make.

'I've been thinking about something over the weekend,' he said.

Angel looked at him curiously. 'Yes, lad?'

'On Friday afternoon, in the canteen, sir,' he said. He looked at Angel again, sheepishly, then looked down. 'There was...there was something...going on.'

'What?' Angel said more loudly and sharply.

'In the canteen, sir,' he said. He hesitated. 'I don't know how to tell you this,' he said. His face showed he regretted having begun the story.

Angel looked up at him and frowned. He had never seen Ahmed like this. He had been on his team for four years and he had not behaved in this way before.

'What is it, lad?' Angel said quietly. 'For goodness sake, spit it out.'

'It's a bit...distasteful, sir. And I am *not* going to name the man...the man who started it. I couldn't do that.'

The muscles round Angel's mouth tightened. 'All right. It's distasteful. Now are you going to tell me or not?'

Ahmed took in a deep breath and said, 'They're taking bets in the canteen on which one is the murderer, sir. I don't know how they found out, but they know that the two men in the cells, Lamb and Franks, and the woman up at the safe house, Margaret Ireland, are the three suspects. They don't seem to know that they are also the possible victims. They asked me about the case. I didn't say anything. I said I had to go, and I came out.'

Angel pursed his lips briefly then said, 'Is *that* all?'

'It's not right, sir. I didn't think they should be taking bets' on people's reputations, sir. Two of those people are innocent, totally innocent, aren't they?'

Angel nodded. 'You're right. But don't let it worry you. I'm sure they mean no harm. The two innocent ones will leave with a clean sheet and be returning to their own homes today, anyway. None of them has been charged. I am expecting the report from the lab at Wetherby, the DNA result on those hairs found on Redman. It will tell us the one we want. Nobody *outside* the station will know that any of them were under suspicion.'

'Right, sir.'

'So don't give it another thought. All right?'

Ahmed breathed out an uneven sigh.

Angel moved on quickly. 'Today's the day that crane will be hoisting the van out of the canal. I want you to liaise with DS Taylor and get a time when they actually expect to make the lift. I want to be there.'

'Right, sir.'

'And tell DS Carter and DS Crisp I want to see them straightaway.'

'It's only just half-past, sir,' he said as he made for the door. Angel's eyes flashed. '*I know. I know,*' he said, 'but there's a lot to do.'

Ahmed blinked. He could see that the inspector was irritable. He would have to be careful. 'Yes, sir,' he said and made for the door.

DS Carter was standing outside in the corridor. She must have just arrived. He stood back and pulled open the door wider.

'The inspector was just asking to see you, Sarge,' he said.

She smiled back at him.

'Yes. Come in, Sergeant,' Angel called.

Ahmed went out and closed the door.

Carter stepped up to the desk.

Angel looked up at her.

She smiled at him sweetly. She was very nicely turned out. He thought she was attractive, too attractive. He wrinkled his nose.

'Did you find anything I'd want to know about in Lamb's house?' Angel said.

'No, sir,' Carter said.

'No new bedsheets or excess of bedsheets, no silver dagger, sandals or laurel bush?'

'No, sir. He has a small garden, but there were no freshly turned-over areas, and no laurel bushes. Though there is a small incinerator at the bottom of the garden. But then, sir, you didn't expect us to find anything incriminating there, because you don't think Lamb is the murderer, do you?'

'I don't know who the murderer is, Sergeant. It still could be him. But I certainly didn't expect him to have left the dagger, the sandals and a pile of bloodstained sheets on the kitchen table waiting for you.'

'Don't worry, sir. We searched the house most thoroughly even though the CCTV apparently didn't convince you it was Lamb stealing the sheets.'

'That's true. I am still not convinced.'

'Yet you haven't had Franks' place searched. Or Margaret Ireland's?'

'I haven't had sufficient justification to present a request for a search warrant of either of their premises. If I had, I would. The business with the CCTV outside the linen shop was more than adequate justification to search Lamb's place. After all, four police officers *thought* that the thief was Lamb.'

Carter's eyes grew bigger in surprise. She thought about it a moment then nodded.

Angel rubbed his chin. Before she could say anything more, he said, 'Ingrid Underwood's daughter is in the interview room at reception. I am very glad she's turned up. See what she wants, apart from the obvious. See if she knows of anybody who would want her mother dead. Find out who would benefit from her mother's death? Any connection with Redman and Peel? Also Lamb, Franks and Margaret Ireland? Did they buy flowers from her mother? See if any of those names ring any bells? Anything that will help to build a case round one of them. Anything in her or her mother's history that might have a bearing on the case? See what you can dig up. Don't overlook anything. All right?'

'Right, sir,' she said and she was gone.

Angel looked after the young woman and rubbed his chin. He would have preferred to have interviewed Rosemary Underwood himself, but she *would* turn up on such a busy day. He sniffed. The decision was made. Carter had to be tested sometime. He pulled out his notes on the back of a used envelope from his inside pocket and began to look down them.

There was a knock at the door. It was Crisp. 'You wanted me, sir?'

'Yes. Come in. Sit down. I want to know about Kenneth Lamb. Did he have alibis for the times of the three murders? And did he have an alibi for the time of the CCTV recording of the sheets being stolen?'

Crisp ran a hand across his lips. 'Well, yes and no, sir.'

Angel's eyes shone and the muscles on his face tightened. 'Explain yourself.'

'His alibi for the time of the murder of Redman, he said that he was at home in bed with his wife. But later, when I spoke to his wife, she said that that night she was away visiting her sister. She spent the night in Stockport, leaving him in the house on his own. Of course, he could simply have got the dates mixed up.'

'So he could have sneaked out of the house, got dressed up in the sheet and sandals, stabbed old Mr Redman and gone back home.'

'Easily, sir. Yes. Now, at the time of the murder of Ingrid Underwood, he would have been on his way to work. If he had the sheet and sandals on him - I don't know where or how he might have changed both in and out of them - but, in terms of time only, he could easily have managed to dash into her shop, stab her and run off. How long did it take, the whole thing? Less than a minute, I should think. He therefore has no alibi for that murder either.'

Angel nodded. He would have to work out how Lamb might have managed the quick change of clothes and the clean up after the murder, but he thought it perfectly possible that he could have committed the murder.

'And what about Angus Peel?'

'Lamb said he finished work at 5.30 and went straight home, sir. His wife said he arrived home at about 6.30, which, if he planned it carefully, gave him sufficient time to stab Peel and dump the van in the canal. Canal Road is almost on his way home from the Coop.'

Angel nodded. It was all very feasible. There were the foundation stones of building a case. Lamb was still very much a suspect.

'Now, what about the time the sheets were being stolen?' Angel said.

Crisp's forehead creased up making more lines than on a charge sheet. He rubbed his chin. 'That was one o'clock last Thursday, sir. He was in a lunchtime meeting in the boardroom at the top of the Coop building with the CEO, the store manager and twelve heads of departments. He's head of Carpets. It's a weekly thing. Lasts about forty minutes. He was definitely there. I saw the store manager and I spoke to the Chief Executive Officer on the phone. They were both quite adamant.'

Angel nearly smiled. He blew out a short breath of self-satisfaction. 'So that's thirteen witnesses to the alibi?'

'Yes, sir.'

'*One* usually suffices,' Angel said.

Crisp suddenly said, 'You said it wasn't him, sir, when we all thought it was. How did you know that?'

'I didn't *know*, lad. But whoever it was, was totally expressionless throughout. He approached the pile of sheets coolly enough, which, from his point of view was exactly as he should have done. Then before making the snatch, I would have expected him to handle the sheet, make sure it would slide of the pile without snagging on anything or causing any disturbance to the display, then I would have expected him to have looked casually around to see who or what might have been observing him, perhaps smiling to put anyone near to him at their ease, but he didn't. He didn't observe any of these natural precautions. He simply made the snatch, shoved the sheet under his coat and made off. And his facial expression remained the same throughout. There was no facial movement whatever. There was not even a flicker of exhilaration at having succeeded or fear at the possibility of being caught. Nothing.'

Crisp had listened attentively to Angel. Now his mouth was slightly open and his eyes fixed on him. He nodded slightly several times. 'So, what's your conclusion then, sir?'

'Well, the thief looked like Lamb. But it wasn't Lamb.'

Crisp looked down and shook his head in disbelief. 'It looked just like him. Everybody said it was Lamb.'

Angel shrugged.

'They say everybody has a doppelganger, sir,' Crisp said. 'Maybe that's what it was.'

Angel pursed his lips then said, 'That would require a triple helping of coincidence, lad, and I don't believe in *that*.'

The phone rang. Angel snatched it up. It was Ahmed.

‘Excuse me, sir. DS Taylor says he expects the van to be hoisted out of the water early this afternoon.’

‘Thank you.’

‘And there’s an envelope for you from Wetherby,’ Ahmed said.

‘*Wetherby*?’ Angel’s heart missed a beat. ‘Well bring it straight through. Don’t waste a second.’

He slammed down the phone and turned to Crisp. ‘The result of the DNA from the lab.’

Crisp’s eyebrows went up.

Angel reached into his desk drawer for the old penknife he kept open and used for opening the post. He sat there poised, knife in hand, ready for the report.

Ahmed knocked, dashed into the office, handed the envelope to Angel and then went back to the door, closed it and stood with his back to it.

Angel slit open the envelope and read the report in a few seconds. His forehead dropped down as he read it again and then handed it to Crisp. Angel’s eyes moved almost imperceptibly as he considered the consequences of the information.

Crisp read the report and lowered it back on to the desk.

There was a silence.

Ahmed looked from one to the other then back to Angel and said, ‘May I ask what it says, sir?’

Angel slowly ran his hand through his hair then said, ‘It essentially says that the DNA sample indicates genes of a female with East Asian heredity, lad.’

Ahmed’s jaw dropped. ‘Margaret Ireland?’ he said.

Crisp said, ‘Does that mean that if Margaret Ireland’s great, great, grandfather or grandmother was from China or Thailand or somewhere like that, then we’ve got her.’

‘Not by itself, no. Her DNA would need to be an identical match to the sample hairs found on the back of Luke Redman’s hand.’

‘That’s soon checked, sir.’

Angel wasn’t pleased. ‘It would take another week.’

The phone rang. Angel glared at it, snatched it up and said, 'Angel.'

It was Harker.

'Come up here. It's urgent,' he said and replaced the phone. It clicked annoyingly in Angel's ear. Angel's lips tightened back against his teeth. The last place in the world he wanted to be at that moment was in Harker's office.

'That's the Super. Wait here. I don't expect to be long.'

Angel stormed up the corridor, his face the same as he'd looked when he'd first smelled Strangeways fish pie.

He knocked on the door and went in.

Harker was at his desk, which was crowded by four piles of papers and files. He was removing the white stick inhaler from his nostril. He raised his eyebrows and said, 'Now then. What about it? Have you had a result from Wetherby? Who is it? That man from the Coop, Kenneth Lamb?'

'Apparently not, sir. The sample has female genes. It could possibly be Margaret Ireland if she has East Asian blood in her genes. The lab needs a sample to be positive.'

'Margaret Ireland? A woman?' He looked straight ahead over the desk at the wall opposite. He was thinking. After a few moments, he shook his head and then said, 'Well, are you going to charge her?'

'It's difficult, sir.'

'Why? Don't you think it's her?'

'I'm not sure. It's difficult to argue with science, but I thought that climbing up a ladder, thrusting a dagger into at least one man - admittedly a man in his eighties - then later, into a woman, a quite healthy, strong woman, had to be the work of an athletic man.'

'Well, by the look of the food bill I've had from the safe house, she eats more than a wing of Wakefield Prison, so don't let her femininity fool you. Have you discovered a motive yet?'

'No, sir.'

'Huh. You are in a mess, aren't you?' Harker said with a smile.

Angel noticed with surprise that he had smiled. It was very unusual. He hardly ever smiled. It was said round the station that every time Harker smiled, a donkey died.

'Better not let your reporters on the tabloids know,' Harker said. 'I expect they'd love to pull you down a peg or two and spoil your record of always getting your man.'

Harker was really enjoying himself, and Angel knew it. There was nothing Angel wanted to say that he *could* say so he had to stand there and take it.

'If you've finished with me, sir, I'd like to get back.'

Harker said, 'I gave you until today and now your time is up.'

'What do you want me to do?'

'You can't continue to use the cells and the safe house as warehousing for potential victims. I told you that.'

'They are also suspects, sir.'

'You can't have a pile of suspects. For god's sake, arrest one of them and send the other two home.'

Angel pulled a face. He was in a vice and he didn't like it.

There were no options left open to him. 'Give me until six o'clock, sir,' he said.

'Five minutes to five. I will be going home at five o'clock and I will want to know who will still be getting free board and lodging before I go.'

*

Angel ran all the way down the green corridor back to his office. He opened the door to find DS Crisp and Ahmed still waiting for him.

He looked straight at Crisp and said, 'Trevor, nip up to the safe house, 11 Beechfield Walk, and bring Margaret Ireland and WPC Baverstock back here. Make it quick. And be careful.'

Crisp blinked, then said, 'Are you arresting her, sir?'

'Not yet. Now buzz off. Time's precious,' he said opening the desk drawer.

'Right, sir,' Crisp said and was gone.

Out of the drawer, he took out a pad of printed forms and a pen and began to fill it in very rapidly. He glanced up at Ahmed. 'This is a request for a search warrant. It's very urgent.' He signed it, folded it, put it in an envelope and handed it to him.

'Take that straight to Doctor Suliman. I'll phone Transport and organize a lift for you. It will pick you up at the front of the station ASAP. Wait for the doctor to sign it, then take bring it straight back to me. All right?'

Ahmed nodded, 'Right, sir.'

*

An hour later, Angel was in Interview Room number 2 sitting next to Trevor Crisp and opposite Margaret Ireland and her solicitor, Samuel Shallow. The red light was on and the recording tape running. Angel had already made the opening statement about the time and who was present and so on.

'I don't know what this is about, Inspector,' Margaret Ireland said. 'I don't know why I need a solicitor. I thought I was in that police house for my safety. That's what I was told...to protect me from a murderer. Now you are treating me like a...a criminal.'

'Not at all. And I'm sorry you may think that this is the case. On the contrary, I still believe that you are in great danger and I want to do everything to keep you alive.'

She shuffled uncomfortably and put her top lip briefly over her bottom lip. 'Now you're frightening me,' she said.

'I don't intend to. I have a series of questions to put to you that I hope will assist us to find the murderer. I hope that you will not be offended by them. Firstly, I need to know where you were on Saturday night, 23 May, through to Sunday morning, the 24.'

'I was at home, of course.'

'You were there all night,' he said, '*on your own*.'

Her eyes flashed angrily. 'Of course I was. I live on my own. I've lived on my own for years. You make living on your own, sound...sound almost indecent.'

'Not at all. It is important that I know the truth, that's all. Your private life is entirely your own affair.'

Her eyes flashed. 'I don't have a *private* life, as you call it. And the use of the word "affair" in that context is not at all...appropriate.'

Angel frowned. This wasn't going well. 'Let us move on to the morning of Wednesday, 27 May, four days later. Where were you then?'

'Ah. Wednesday,' she said, then suddenly her face changed. Her eyes darted in various directions before settling on Angel. 'Why are you asking me where I was?' she said. 'What does it matter where I was? Who wants to know? Am I being accused of something? It's these murders, isn't it? You must be thinking that I could be this nutcase character who dresses like a Roman 2000 years ago. Me. Of all people. The most ordinary, respectable, quiet woman in Bromersley. You must be mad, stark staring mad.'

'No,' Angel said. 'Not at all. I have had to ask several other people the same question. It's a matter of knowing where everybody significant in the case was at the critical time. It's a bit like setting out a chess board to find out where all the pieces were at a particular stage in the game, that's all.'

Margaret Ireland rubbed her chin for a measured five seconds then said, 'Very well. I was at home, all Wednesday morning, Inspector. No. Nobody can verify it. Nobody came. Nothing happened. No tradesman delivered anything.'

Angel nodded. 'Thank you.'

'What's your next question?' she said quickly.

'The same thing, the following day, Thursday, Miss Ireland. Where were you in the evening between 5 p.m. and 7 p.m.?'

'The same answer. I was at home. Next?'

Angel rubbed his chin. In a strange sort of way, he was worried for her. 'Think carefully, I urge you, Miss Ireland.

Are you absolutely certain that you saw nobody? Waved at them through the window? Took in a parcel for a neighbour? Paid the milkman? Anything like that?'

'No. No. I don't think so. Come on, let's get on with it. What's your next question?'

'Do you drive a car?'

Her eyebrows went up. 'Why on earth would you want to know that? I *did* drive. I had a beautiful Rover car but, when I retired two years ago, I stopped driving and sold the car. I thought walking would be good for me. And so it has proved to be. Any more questions?'

'Just a few, Miss Ireland. Easy ones. Where were you born?'

The eyebrows went up again. 'Good gracious. I was born in Huddersfield. In the maternity hospital there.'

'And your father and mother, are they Huddersfield people?'

'Of course.'

'And what's their address?'

She gave Angel a sideways glance and said, 'Why do you want to know *that*?'

'Please answer the question, Miss Ireland.'

'Why do you want to know where they live?'

He shrugged. 'Just routine.'

'I wouldn't want you worrying them, Inspector. They're quiet, respectable folk. They could be quite put out by the presence of burly policemen stamping up their garden path.'

'Don't worry, Miss Ireland. It may not be necessary to visit them, but I do need it for my records.'

She was not all pleased. Her face was as friendly as Dartmoor prison in a thunderstorm. Her slim nostrils quivered in response to her heavy breathing.

He sat there, looking at her, his pen poised over the brown envelope.

She ran her hand through her hair and said, 'If you insist, it is 121 Lumb Lane, Huddersfield.'

'Thank you very much, and there's just one more thing for now.'

'Anything to get this over with.'

He reached into his jacket pocket and took out a small plastic polythene envelope.

'Could I have two or three hairs straight from your head?' She stared hard at him, her eyes were as cold as icicles from the prison roof.

*

DS Taylor in a loud voice said, 'Divers, out of the water, please.'

DS Maroney and DC Cutts of Leeds Police Underwater Team waded to the side of the canal and hoisted themselves on to the bank next to where Angel was standing.

They removed the nose clips, lifted their goggles, and turned off their oxygen tanks. They greeted Angel, who nodded back.

'Right, Clem, take the tension,' Taylor called out to the crane driver.

The big man in the jockey cap positioned a lever and held on to it as he slowly let in the clutch. The slack wires at each corner of the submerged van whipped the surface of the water then straightened out and became taut.

The crane engine began to groan as it worked to release the van wheels from centuries of mud and junk that had formed the floor of the old canal. As the engine laboured, the crane began to tilt precariously towards the water.

Angel looked at the crane driver but he seemed not to be alarmed. The driver held on to the lever and maintained a steady strain.

The angle of the crane settled, but it shuddered occasionally on the heavy steel framework specially built for it on the far bank of the canal.

After ten or fifteen minutes, Angel could see the white van under the water drift a little away from the bridge, before it drifted back and the white roof edged unevenly through the surface of the water, causing a slight ripple.

There were murmurs of rejoicing from the small crowd of police and other observers.

The water under the bridge became black and ebbed and flowed through the weeds, throwing up lager cans, washing-up liquid bottles, women's tights, part of an HMV radio casing and other litter not possible to identify.

Progress was slower than a judge's summing up. After half an hour, only 10 inches of one corner of the van roof was visible.

Angel looked at his watch. This was wasting valuable time. His mobile phone rang. It was Ahmed. 'I've got that warrant to search Margaret Ireland's, sir.'

'Is DS Crisp there?'

'I'll find him, sir.'

'Go on then, lad. I'll hold on.'

Two minutes later Crisp was on the line.

Angel said, 'Ah, Trevor, I want you to find DS Carter and take her and Ahmed to Margaret Ireland's house. Ahmed's got the warrant. Meet you there.'

Angel closed the phone, dropping it in his pocket as he made his way down the bank to his car.

He was soon on Wakefield Road making his way up the hill towards the town centre. Five minutes later, he pulled on to the Willows Estate. He saw Trevor Crisp's car outside a small semi-detached house. He pulled up behind it, tried the door of the house and found it locked so he rang the doorbell. Ahmed let him in. The team had already started the search. The house was searched methodically and all supposed secret hiding places were checked. Police search teams were well used to finding hiding places. They took down mirrors held in place by screws with cosmetic heads to see if a cavity had been created behind. They removed the sides of the boxed-in bath to see what might be concealed in the space around the bath. They checked for loose floorboards under fitted carpets that had had tacks removed at a corner. All upstairs floors were carefully walked across to check for any sense of a loose floorboard. The stairs were measured on the underside to see if a secret space had been created. Nothing was overlooked.

DS Carter had been in the dining room looking through the sideboard drawers and had discovered, underneath a surfeit of tablecloths, a large folder inside which was a photograph album and several loose photographs. She opened the folder on the table and was surprised at what she saw.

She went out to the kitchen and said to Angel. 'You might want to see these photographs, sir.'

Angel followed her into the dining room. 'What is it, Sergeant?'

Carter turned the pages of photographs of Margaret Ireland taken in her late teens or early twenties. It seems it was a portfolio for a model agency. Some of the photographs showed her wearing only the tiniest bits of lace.

'A bit bold for the 1980s, sir?' Carter said.

Angel had to concur, but she looked very beautiful. There was a photograph of her in a skimpy Roman-style dress as the character Aristana, the teenage nymphomaniac in the production of *Nero*. There was also one of her with Malcolm Malloy. They were in full costume and make-up and had their arms round each other in what purported to be a loving embrace. Angel assumed it would have been a publicity photograph for the play. There was also a rather a more staid photograph of her with Luke Redman. She was on a pseudo-marble seat and he was standing behind her with his hand on her shoulder which Angel thought intended to convey an avuncular relationship. And there was a copy of the same photograph Angel had found on Redman's study wall of the entire cast and production staff of the play.

Angel rubbed his chin. At length he said, 'Thank you. Very interesting. Pack them up and put them back as they were.'

He returned to the kitchen. He wasn't certain whether the sight of Margaret Ireland's photographs would advance his inquiries or not. It highlighted the fact that there were no photographs of any family members or friends in the collection or indeed anywhere in the house. He meandered through the hall into the kitchen where Ahmed was searching. He noticed that the key was in the back door lock so he turned it and went out into the rear garden. It was well kept but there were no signs of recently disturbed earth. He came back inside and locked the door.

The team concluded their search and, having found nothing incriminating, they congregated in the kitchen. They couldn't hide their disappointment.

Crisp said, 'What are you going to do then, sir?'

Angel sighed, then said, 'We have nothing to hold either of the two men, even though neither of them has an alibi for any of the murders. I am loath to return them to their respective homes, but I have no choice. Margaret Ireland has no alibis either, but the DNA result is enough to hold her for questioning.'

'Seems very unfair, sir,' Carter said.

Angel nodded. 'It is unfair.' He turned to Crisp. 'When you've finished here, go to the station, see Lamb and tell him that Superintendent Harker is unwilling to provide him with police security after 4.55 p.m. today.'

Crisp's eyebrows shot up. 'Can I say that, sir?'

'It's the truth, lad,' Angel said. 'You can.'

Angel then turned to Carter and said, 'And you say the same thing to Franks.'

Carter looked surprised.

Angel continued, 'Then you ask them to vacate the cells and suggest that they leave town, stay with a relation or in a hotel quietly somewhere until we catch the murderer. Tell nobody of their location but let me have their phone number. The mobile number would be best for security reasons. If they are careful about it, it will keep them safe. All right?'

'What if anything should happen to either of them?' Carter said.

'It shouldn't if they are careful,' Angel said.

Carter looked at Crisp and then at Angel and said, 'Superintendent Harker *has* given you an ultimatum, hasn't he, sir?'

Angel nodded. 'He's my boss. I have to do as he says or leave the force. The same as you have to. All right?'

Carter and Crisp exchanged glances.

There was a short silence. Nobody seemed to know what to say.

Ahmed seized the opportunity to join in the conversation, and eased his way between the two sergeants and said, 'Excuse me, sir. If Margaret Ireland is the murderer, then what is her motive?'

Angel rubbed his chin. 'Ask me a question I *can* answer, lad. It's certain that there's no logic to these murders. There's no discernible motive,' he said, glad to be able to change the subject. 'There is no money, gold, prize, estate, glory or lover to win. The murderer is simply feeding his or her ego, or exacting revenge. Or, it may be something else that is totally obscure. That's why it is so difficult to solve. We are clearly dealing with someone who is sick. A psychopath. A lunatic. Somebody totally unhinged. *They* are the most difficult of all to catch. They are always bolder, cleverer and more dangerous than your average murderer, also they are inclined to play games with their adversaries. I expect he or she is doing exactly that with us right now. They act normally to the outside world, but privately, in their own minds, they are acting out a bizarre existence.'

'How do you catch them, sir,' Ahmed said.

Angel's eyebrows shot up. 'They *can* be caught by slogging, thorough police work, but also by thinking like they do.'

'How do you do that,' Ahmed said.

Angel frowned. Then gripped his chin between thumb and two fingers, pursed his lips and said, 'I don't know. I really don't know. I expect it comes in time.'

'Are you doing it now, sir?'

'I'm trying to,' he said. 'I'm trying to. But there's something I must have missed. There must be. I don't know what it is.' Then he suddenly looked at his watch and said, 'I have to go.'

He made for the door, then turned round and looked at them all.

'Finish up here,' he said. 'If you find anything, phone me. I'm going back to the station briefly. Then I'm going down to Canal Road.'

'Right, sir,' they called in unison. He waved in response and was gone.

He drove straight to the station and phoned Mr Twelvetrees at the CPS about Margaret Ireland. He read him the DNA report on the hairs found on Luke Redman, pointing out that the sample indicated genes of a female with East Asian heredity. He told him that Margaret Ireland had no alibi for any of the three murders, that she was one of the last three people alive and involved in the production of *Nero*, but added that there was no other direct evidence against her. Then he asked Twelvetrees if there was enough evidence to charge her with the murders. The barrister said that it was his opinion that there was not enough evidence circumstantial or otherwise to arrest and charge her for murder, but that there was definitely sufficient evidence to hold her for forty-eight hours for further questioning. That suited Angel admirably. He thanked him, rang off and immediately tapped in Taylor's number.

'Is the van out of the water yet, Don?'

'Yes, sir. It's tented and Dr Mac's working on the body. It will take us a bit longer because the crime scene, of course, is significantly spoiled.'

'Have you been inside the van?'

'Yes, sir. Just about finished the inside. I came out for a breather. The smell is...unspeakable.'

'What have you found?'

'Well, sir, the ignition key was switched on and a long length of 2" by 1" timber was jammed between the seat back and the accelerator pedal.'

Angel had expected that or something similar. 'Was there anything in the van, such as a mirror?'

‘I thought you’d ask about a mirror, sir. No. But on the windscreen in red paint was the message: “III to go”.’

Angel’s face muscles tightened and his heart beat faster. Although the message was entirely predictable, he felt that the audacious killer was speaking directly to him. He knew it and he didn’t like it.

‘Right, Don,’ he said. ‘That’s enough for now. Is Mac there?’

‘He’s just coming out of the tent, sir. Hold on.’

Angel heard some unintelligible exchanges between them, there was a pause, then he heard Mac’s broad Glaswegian voice. ‘Now then Michael, what you wantin’ from me?’

‘Tell me straight, Mac. Is the wound on that victim, Peel, the same as the ones on Luke Redman and Ingrid Underwood?’

‘Aye. It is. And I believe it to have been made by the same weapon, a dagger with a 6” blade.’

‘No laurel leaf?’

Mac snorted. ‘Give me a chance. There’s a laurel leaf tucked inside his shirt lapel. That’s all you what you wanted to know, isn’t it?’

CHAPTER TWELVE

There was a knock at the door.

Angel looked up. 'Come in,' he said.

It was WPC Baverstock. 'We've got Margaret Ireland for you, sir,' she said. 'Did you want her here or in an interview room?'

'In here, for the minute,' Angel said.

'In here, Miss Ireland, please,' Baverstock said.

The woman came in. She looked round the office then down at Angel. She didn't look pleased.

DC Scrivens followed close behind and closed the door.

Margaret Ireland looked from Angel to Scrivens to Baverstock and then back to Angel. 'I'm not used to being moved around from place to place like a parcel,' she said.

'I'm transferring you to a cell in the station,' Angel said.

She blinked. She was obviously surprised. 'It will be safer here, I suppose,' she said.

Angel nodded. 'Not only that, Mrs Ireland, but in view of certain forensic evidence there is some possibility that it may be necessary for you to have to explain your presence in Luke Redman's bedroom the night he was murdered. In the meantime, I am holding you for further questioning.'

Her eyes almost popped out of her head. '*What?*' she said. 'Luke Redman's bedroom? Ridiculous. That stupid old man was old enough to be my grandfather! I wouldn't be seen dead with him. What are you up to, Inspector?'

'There's no need for you to offer any explanation now,' Angel said. 'I suggest that you consult your solicitor and I'll speak to you tomorrow. All right?'

'No. It is not all right. I wouldn't be seen dead with the stupid old fool. I don't know what strange ideas you have got hold of, Inspector, or what cock and bull evidence you have concocted, but it's utterly ridiculous and outrageous.'

Angel looked up at Baverstock and said, 'Take her down to the cells. See that she has all that she needs.'

'Right, sir.'

As they went out, the phone rang.

Angel reached out for it. It was Harker.

'Do you know the time.'

'*Yes*, sir. It's 4.55,' he said. He knew full well what the time was, and he told the superintendent what he wanted to hear.

Harker grunted, said, 'That's better,' and put the receiver down.

Angel was about as happy as a villain who expected an ASBO and got two years.

Thank god it was time to go home.

There was a knock at the door. He looked up and sneered across at it.

'Come in.'

It was Carter.

'Oh, yes,' he said, suddenly brightening. 'How did Tom Franks take the news? Was he put out at all?'

'He was surprised, sir.'

He looked at her closely. 'Did he show any signs of...of reluctance...or fear?'

'He seemed unhappy at losing police protection, but glad to leave the cell. I must say, sir, I think you are taking a great risk withdrawing protection like this.'

He heard her clear enough. He didn't choose to reply.

'Did he mention that he had a suitable hideaway to go to?'

'He didn't say, sir. But he did say that he was packing a bag and leaving immediately.'

'Did he give you a mobile phone number?'

'Yes, sir.'

She passed a card with a handwritten number on it. He raised his eyebrows, glanced at the card and then put it in his pocket. 'I assume there was nothing to report about Ingrid Underwood's daughter, Rosemary?'

'Nothing vital, sir, or I would have said. Things *have* been moving on rather quickly.'

Angel nodded.

'Anyway, sir, Rosemary Underwood said that she knew of no one who would wish her mother dead. She said that, as she was the only child, she was the only one to benefit financially from her mother's death. Her mother divorced years ago and she can't remember her father. She knows of no connection between her mother and Luke Redman or Angus Peel, and the names, Kenneth Lamb, Tom Franks and Margaret Ireland meant nothing at all to her, and she doesn't know if any of them had been customers and bought flowers from her mother at any time. She didn't know anything about the production of *Nero* either. The only relationship of her mother's she knew of - and she didn't like it - was the man opposite who has the bike shop, Carl Young. And that's about it, sir.'

'What didn't Rosemary like about him?'

'Nothing specific, sir. She said he was always hanging around when she visited her mother at the shop.'

Angel frowned, closed his eyes for a second, then said, 'He fancied her, that's all. She wasn't bad looking. I bet she'd been a cracker twenty years ago. Kids are always jealous. Anything else?'

Carter nodded in agreement and then said, 'No, sir. I think I've covered everything.'

Angel nodded. He pursed his lips then rubbed his chin. She appeared to have done a thorough job interviewing Rosemary Underwood. She had asked all the questions he would have asked. He was wondering whether he wanted her to accompany him on a visit to Margaret Ireland's parents. Ron Gawber, his sergeant for ten years, would have been the ideal copper to have sent on that sort of job on his own. Alas, he was not available to him anymore.

'About Margaret Ireland,' he said. 'There are so many reasons why she is probably *not* the murderer we are seeking. I really need some hard evidence to charge her or make a decision to eliminate her completely, before Kenneth Lamb or Tom Franks is found dead.'

Carter looked surprised. 'She's in a cell, sir. Isn't she?'

'Yes. For only forty-eight hours, then I'll have to release her. She's not been charged with murder. She can't be, yet. Not enough evidence. The only hard clue we have is the DNA on the two hairs found on the back of Luke Redman's hand.'

'Aren't you waiting for a DNA result on the hair you took from her yesterday?'

'That'll take a few days. She'll be out before then, and if she's the murderer and she finds Lamb or Franks, it will be god help them. The lab said that the gene pattern indicates the hair belonged to a female of East Asian origin. If Margaret Ireland's parents or forbears are East Asian, then she must be the murderer. She's the only female it *could* be.'

Carter nodded.

'First thing in the morning,' Angel said, 'we'll visit her parents.'

'Right, sir.'

There was a knock at the door.

Angel's eyebrows went up. 'See who it is, will you?'

She opened the door.

A voice said, 'Ah, Flora, is the boss in?'

It was DS Crisp. Angel recognized his voice.

'Come in,' he said, then to Carter he said, 'Push off home. See you here, first thing in the morning.'

She went out and closed the door.

'Did you see Lamb off all right?'

'He said he was pleased to go. He was bored to tears and the place hadn't the comforts of home,' Crisp said.

'Did he give you a mobile number?'

'No, sir.'

Angel's hands tightened into fists. 'It wasn't supposed to be the Dorchester,' he said. 'It was to save his skin. Where's he going to go undercover? The Maldives?'

'I don't believe he's planning to go anywhere, sir. He said he'll take his chances.'

Angel ran his tongue along his lower lip. He was thinking. He was glad he didn't have Superintendent Harker's conscience. 'You're sure that he understood the risk?'

'He said he wasn't scared of anything.'

'What's his home address?' Angel said as he reached out for the phone.

'72 Wentworth View, sir. On the corner. What are you doing?'

Eventually a voice in the earpiece said, 'Inspector Asquith.'

'Michael Angel here, Haydn.'

'Oh, the scruffy branch of her majesty's constabulary,' Asquith quipped. 'What can I do for you?'

Angel didn't mind the friendly jibe if he could get his own way. 'It's more what I can do for you, Haydn. I have an idea that there might be a burglary at 72 Wentworth View tonight. If you could get your lads to keep an eye on the place...? Use the street corner as a rendezvous point a few times in the night. You know the sort of thing?'

'Certainly watch that, my son. Have no fear. Thanks for the tip-off, Michael. If my lads can make a collar, they will. There'll be no robbery there tonight, I can assure you. Pleasant dreams.'

He replaced the phone.

Crisp looked at Angel, smiled and shook his head knowingly.

Angel wasn't smiling. He was rubbing his chin in thought.

'There's one loose end that has not been cleared up, Trevor,' Angel said. 'I want you to see to it tomorrow morning, while I'm in Huddersfield with the new sergeant. It's the business with Cyril Krill and that Solar Heating and Power Exhibition in London last week. Krill originally said that he went down there alone, yet in the fair's visitor's book, the organizer told DS Carter that he had arrived there with a woman and signed in as Mr and Mrs Krill. Now, you know all about Mrs Krill. You interviewed her.'

'Yes, sir. She spent the weekend at home with a migraine.'

'Aye. I don't know what we can do about that, lad. A migraine without a witness is not an alibi. Anyway, you remember, you were with me when Krill told us about a relationship he had had with a woman whose name he can't remember; it began with an "M". We never did tidy that up, such a lot happening. But I hadn't forgotten it. I want you to go back to him. Lean on him. Take Scrivens with you. I want you to get him to produce an alibi for the Saturday night/Sunday morning his father-in-law was murdered, if he can. Then I want you check it out, thoroughly. If it doesn't hold up, bring him in for questioning. He's probably got a strong enough motive to have murdered the old man, but, of course, we have no evidence against him in respect of Ingrid Underwood nor Angus Peel. However, it should make him sit up and take us seriously. He can't play ducks and drakes with us like that.'

'Right, sir.'

*

'Good morning, sir,' Carter said as she pulled open the door of Angel's BMW.

Angel nodded and, as the door closed, he let in the clutch and the car pulled smartly away from the steps of Bromersley Police Station and headed for Huddersfield Road and over the moors. They hardly spoke through the short journey.

Eventually Angel said, 'We need to find out if Margaret Ireland has any Far Eastern heritage. If she has, it would be a step nearer to matching the DNA of the hair and provide justification for arresting her and charging her with the three murders.'

'So you want me to keep a lookout for anything Chinese or Japanese or - similar?'

'It's a matter of confirmation or elimination.'

It didn't take long to reach Huddersfield town centre.

He handed Carter the street guide. 'Lumb Lane is off the road to Oldham,' Angel said.

And so it was: a very long back street of terraced houses, which had their front doors opening directly on to the pavement. He found number 121 and was able to stop and park the BMW right outside the front door. Two little girls with skinny white arms and legs were bouncing balls against the red brick walls of a nearby house.

Angel knocked on the door panel and waited.

Angel and Carter exchanged looks. He knocked again and the door was opened five inches and an elderly man's voice said, 'What is it? What do you want?'

'Mr Ireland?'

'Yes. What is it?'

They pulled out their ID cards and Angel said, 'I'm Inspector Angel and this is Sergeant Carter. We want to talk to you about your daughter, Margaret.'

'What about her?' he said opening the door another two inches. 'She's all right, isn't she? Has something happened to her?'

A woman's voice from inside said, 'What is it? What do they want? We don't want to change our gas again.'

The old man turned his head. 'It's the police. About Margaret.'

'*Margaret*!' the woman yelled. 'The police? What's happened?'

Angel said, 'Can we come in?'

The door was yanked wide open.

'Come in,' the old lady said. 'Go through. Find a seat. Sit anywhere. I'm her mother. What's this all about? There'll be a man behind it. There always is. Didn't I say so?' she said, looking at her husband.

Angel and Carter were quickly ushered through the tiny front room to the tinier kitchen at the back. Angel glanced round the rooms for photographs. There were no photographs anywhere to be seen.

When everybody was settled, the old lady stared at Angel and said, 'Well? Speak up young man. What's happened?'

Angel said, 'Have you not been in touch with your daughter lately?'

She looked away from him. 'At Christmas she phoned us and sent us a card and a plant in a pot. Why?'

'It was a poinsettia. It was very beautiful,' Mr Ireland said.

She glared at her husband and said, 'It died after two weeks.'

He nodded, then said, 'Well, nothing lasts forever.'

Angel jumped in quickly and said, 'You haven't been in touch since?'

Mrs Ireland said, 'She knows our phone number.'

'And we have hers,' Mr Ireland said. 'And a telephone works in both directions.'

Mrs Ireland turned on him. 'You be quiet. You don't know what you're saying.' Then she looked at Angel and said, 'Take no notice of him. He doesn't know what he's saying. He's got Alzheimer's.'

'I've *not* got Alzheimer's,' Ireland said.

She looked at Angel, shrugged and said, 'You see. He's forgotten what the doctor said already. I have to live with this.'

'You probably won't be aware that there's been a series of murders in Bromersley over the past two weeks and I believe that your daughter is on the murderer's list.'

Mrs Ireland's pale face went whiter than the outside lavatory walls. 'Oh my lovely daughter. Is she all right?'

'She's absolutely safe,' Angel said. 'She's in Bromersley Police Station.'

'Oh thank you. Thank you. Thank you very much. Will she be safe there?'

Mr Ireland looked at her, shook his head and said, 'You can't get safer in this country than a police station, Thelma.'

'What do *you* know?' she said. 'All those policemen. They're all *men*.'

Carter said, 'They're all highly dedicated men *and* women on the Bromersley force, Mrs Ireland. You need have no worries there.'

Ireland looked at his wife and said, 'I told you.'

'Shut up, you,' she said. 'You don't know anything.'

Angel explained the murder case and the involvement of their daughter to the Irelands, who were surprised that they had not known about it. They remembered that their daughter had had a part in the *Nero* production twenty years earlier and that they had expressed their disapproval of the subject matter and the role their daughter had been cast to play. They remembered the fire, that the play had been called off, and that a young man had died, but little else. Angel did not explain the true reason for his visit.

'And what can we do to help,' Mr Ireland said.

Before Angel could reply, Mrs Ireland, the corners of her mouth turned down and her nose wrinkled up, said, 'I'm her mother, Inspector. Only a mother understands. She's my only child. I don't know what I've done to deserve a daughter like her. I made such sacrifices to send her to a good school and then university. I had such high hopes for her. And she was so very beautiful. She was a highly successful model. In great demand. Then she had relationships with several dreadful men that all turned to nought. I thought she would get married and provide me with a grandchild, or more than one, but she never did. Took up a job teaching. Then moved away. Don't see her from one year to another now. Virtually abandoned me. Left me to struggle on in my old age. It's not a bit right.'

'If you didn't go on at her so much when she *did* come, she'd come more often,' Ireland said.

She glared at him and said, 'Shut up you. You don't know. Only a mother understands.' She turned to Angel and said, 'He doesn't understand. He doesn't remember what went on. He's got Alzheimer's.'

Ireland leaped up from the stool. 'Haven't got Alzheimer's,' he yelled. He turned to Angel and said, 'I haven't got Alzheimer's, Inspector. She's the one with Alzheimer's. She doesn't know what she's saying half the time.'

Mrs Ireland's face reddened. 'Ernest Ireland, you are telling lies. You're the one with the Alzheimer's.' She turned to Angel, 'Excuse him, Inspector. He doesn't know what he's saying. A few years ago, they would have taken him off in a straitjacket, locked him up in Storthes Hall and thrown away the key. Now he's filled up with pills and stays at home, and I have to put up listening to him spouting gibberish all day.'

Angel said, 'Where did you two meet?'

'Atkinson's Mill, two miles down the road,' Ireland said.

'I was a chargehand,' Mrs Ireland said, 'he was the lavatory man.'

Ireland's eyes popped out of his head. 'I was *not* the lavatory man. I was on maintenance.'

'It was your job to keep them clean and working.'

'That was only *one* of my jobs. My job mostly comprised keeping the bobbins spinning - the machines *you* worked on.'

Angel ran his hand through his hair. 'You were both born round here then?'

'I was born two streets away, on Paradise Street,' she said. 'He was born in Halifax.'

'I was born in Elland, dammit,' he said.

'You always said in the hospital in Halifax,' she said. Then she looked at Angel, held up her hands in a hopeless gesture and said, 'You see. He's not right in the head. For more than forty-five years he's always said he was born in Halifax. Now since he was diagnosed with Alzheimer's, he's forgotten...suddenly he's born in Elland.'

'I was always born in Elland. It's you that forgets everything, Thelma. I always said Elland. It's never been any different. Which reminds me, have you taken your pills?'

'No, I haven't but they're nothing to do with my brain. They're for...down below. I'm as quick as ever I was.'

Angel looked down at her and said, 'You lived with your parents on Paradise Street.'

'My father, mother, grandmother and five sisters.'

'Quite a houseful,' Angel said. 'What was your mother's maiden name?'

'Armitage,' she said. Her eyes shone with pleasure at her prompt reply. 'Ask me any question you like, Inspector. You won't catch *me* out. My brain's like quicksilver.'

Angel nodded. 'And what was *your* maiden name?'

'Wilson. My name before I married *him* was, Thelma Grace Wilson.'

'And what about your husband's family?' Angel said.

Ireland said, 'I can answer for myself. And I can answer just as quickly as she can.'

Angel looked at him and said, 'What was your mother's maiden name?'

'Beaumont,' he said.

'That's right,' Mrs Ireland said.

Ireland glared at her. She pulled a face at him and then turned away.

Angel licked his lips. This wasn't progressing his inquiries at all. These were all well-known local names.

'Don't you have any exciting, exotic names in your history?' he said.

'Like what?' she said.

'Well...foreign names,' he said, watching for their reaction.

They frowned, looked at each other, then in unison said, 'No.'

Angel had another idea.

'Interesting,' he said. 'Do you have any photographs of the old folk?'

'What do you mean?' she said.

'Your parents or your grandparents?'

'No,' she replied.

'That's correct. She got *that* right,' Mr Ireland said.

Angel rubbed his chin. If the Irelands had any secrets, they were certainly keeping them to themselves.

CHAPTER THIRTEEN

After Angel had turned the BMW round and was heading back to Bromersley, he turned to Carter and said, 'I can't see anything East Asian about Margaret Ireland.'

'No, sir,' she said. 'And I understand why she doesn't visit her mum and dad that often.'

'That means that she is no longer the prime suspect. We will have to await the lab comparison DNA of her hair sample to be absolutely positive. As she is the only female suspect, I don't know where to go from here. There aren't many women in this case and we've no evidence against any of them. You interviewed Rosemary Underwood. What are your thoughts about her?'

'I know we shouldn't trust our opinion, but I honestly can't think a lightweight young woman like Rosemary Underwood could stick a dagger into an old man, her mother and a man in a van. It's a crime you would expect a man to commit.'

'True, but the DNA has never been wrong, in my experience. And there is no possibility that the crime scene could have been contaminated. I would trust both DS Taylor and Dr Mac with my life.'

There was a pause.

'What are we going to do then, sir?'

'It means retracing our steps. Looking at everybody, particularly the female of the species.'

There was another pause.

'You interviewed Kathleen Krill, sir. What did you make of her?'

'A strong minded woman. I suppose if she had the motivation...yes, I suppose she could have committed the murders.'

They came up to the thirty-mile-an-hour restriction sign, and the town boundary sign announcing that they were in Bromersley.

Angel slowed the BMW to thirty mph and said, 'But there's something wrong. I can't put my finger on it, but there's something very wrong.'

Carter wondered whether to ask him to explain. She thought if he wanted to, he would do. She waited. Nothing more was forthcoming.

When they arrived in his office, on his desk there was SOCO's report on Ronnie Striker's jeans, T-shirt and trainers. Angel read it and reread it then passed it to Carter.

Angel said, 'It says that his clothes were clean. There were no signs of Ingrid Underwood's blood.'

'Yes, sir,' she said as she put the report down.

He rubbed his chin then suddenly said, 'Tomorrow morning, if the sun is shining brightly and there is little or no cloud, I want you and Ahmed and Ronnie Striker to be at Ingrid Underwood's shop at 8.40 sharp. Will you lay that on? And go gently with Ronnie Striker. Remember, he only has the emotional capacity and control of a twelve-year-old boy.'

She frowned. 'Only if the sun is shining brightly -'

'And there is no cloud, yes.'

'Right, sir,' she said. She went out and closed the door.

He pulled open the desk drawer and took out a silver-plated paper knife. He had never used it for that purpose. In fact, he had never used it for any purpose. He had had the thing that long he couldn't remember how he came by it. It was in the shape of a miniature sword. He crossed to the window and held it briefly in the sunlight and watched it reflect the sun's rays. Then he dropped it in his pocket and thoughtfully returned to his desk.

The phone rang. It was Crisp.

'I saw Krill first thing this morning, sir. He messed around again in the beginning but when he saw we meant business he came clean. His marriage is about over, but he didn't want his wife Kathleen to find out about his relationship with another woman, an actress called Nadine Ellerman.'

'Who? Never heard of her.'

'She's registered with Equity. I've checked. The address also checks out. He says he met her in London on Saturday afternoon and never left her side. He did take her to the exhibition, and they stayed together until he left her on Monday afternoon, 25 May to return to Sheffield.'

'If she confirms it, he's off the hook.'

'She *has* confirmed it, sir. I've just seen her. At her flat in Gloucester Road.'

Angel blinked. 'Where are you now?'

'In a taxi, sir, on the way to Kings Cross.'

Angel's face went the colour of a judge's robe. '*In a taxi*? *In London*? Do you think you're on your holidays? Have you gone mad?'

'I thought this...this inquiry was urgent, sir,' Crisp said.

It *was* urgent. Extremely urgent. Lines of inquiry in this case were rapidly coming to a close.

'It *is* urgent,' Angel said, 'but don't milk the situation. The underground was good enough for me, it should be good enough for you. You're not Condoleezza Rice on a mission to save the world, you know. And none of those British Rail afternoon teas on your way home, else I'll be in hock to the Super for years.'

'I'm only doing what I thought you wanted,' Crisp said.

Angel knew better. He ran his hand through his hair. 'That's that then. Come on back and see what you can do with Kathleen Krill. A migraine without a witness is not an alibi. Go and see her. Maybe she had a phone call or something? Or maybe there is a link between her and Ingrid Underwood and Angus Peel.'

'Right, sir. I'll give it a go.'

'Take Scrivens with you, just to be on the safe side.'

*

'Good morning, sir.'

'Good morning everybody,' Angel said as he got out of the BMW. He crossed the pavement, pushed a key into the door of Ingrid Underwood's shop, unlocked it, but didn't go in. He stood on the pavement, looked at Carter, Ahmed and Ronnie Striker in turn and said, 'It is exactly a week today since Ingrid Underwood was murdered. The time of the murder was between 8.40 and nine o'clock. It is exactly 8.40 now. The sun is shining brightly, as it was that day. I want to re-enact the scene as it happened then.'

Angel pushed open the door and went inside. It smelled strongly of foliage and blossom from years of housing and preparing flowers. A strong ray of sunlight cut through the shop from a back window, illuminating the dust.

He turned to Carter. Will you be Ingrid Underwood? I want you to position yourself on your back behind the workbench, your feet towards the door.'

'Right, sir,' she said and made towards the bench.

'Ahmed, I want you to be the...one with the dagger,' he said, and he reached into his pocket and pulled out the miniature sword paperknife which he thrust into his hand.

'Now then, Ronnie,' Angel said. 'Firstly, tell me, when you arrived here back from the sandwich shop was this door open or closed?'

'It was open,' Ronnie Striker said.

'You said that Mrs Underwood used a brick to prop it open. Is it there?'

He rummaged round the back of the shop door and found it. It was covered in silver dust. He held it up surprised.

Angel saw him and said, 'It's aluminium powder. It's what we use to look for fingerprints.'

Striker nodded and put it in position, so that the door was wide open.

'Thank you. Now, Ronnie, can you tell me...is DS Carter in the position Mrs Underwood was?'

'Yes.'

'And where was ... Jesus?'

'He was on his knees, leaning over her.'

Angel tossed his head to Ahmed to tell him to take up that position.

Ahmed tentatively knelt at the side of DS Carter and looked back at Angel.

'Like that?' Angel said.

'He was closer.'

Ahmed hesitated.

Angel said, 'Go on, lad. Hutch up. Sergeant Carter doesn't mind.'

Ahmed slowly took up the position.

Carter looked up at him and smiled.

Angel said, 'Is that it as it was, Ronnie?'

'Yes.'

'Ahmed, hold up the paperknife in your right hand.'

He did so and the sharp ray of sunshine through the rear window caught the paperknife, creating a brilliant white reflection.

Angel was expecting it, but Ronnie Striker was not and he gasped with surprise at seeing the sight again.

'Twist your wrist about, Ahmed.'

The movement caused the reflections to shimmer.

'There's your star, Ronnie,' Angel said.

Ronnie Striker saw the effect, stuffed his hands in his pockets, turned away and looked down towards the floor.

Angel turned to him and said, 'Never mind. It was an understandable mistake. Thanks for coming. I'll get Sergeant Carter to take you straight home now.'

Ronnie Striker didn't reply. He ran outside and stood by the Ford.

Angel turned to Carter and Ahmed. 'Thanks very much, you two,' Angel said. 'You can get up now.'

CHAPTER FOURTEEN

Angel made it straight back to his office. He had just settled at his desk when there was a knock at the door. It was Taylor and he was carrying a length of timber. Angel peered at it.

'I've finished the examination of Angus Peel's van, sir,' Taylor said.

'That's great, Don.'

'I'm afraid there's not much that you will want to hear, sir.'

'So tell me anyway.'

'Well, there aren't any prints on any of the door handles, the steering wheel, the gear stick, or the ignition key - the obvious places. They've been wiped clean or the murderer wore gloves. And I can't rely on any of the many samples in the mud that had floated on to his clothes, his shoes, his head and his hands. They could have originated from anywhere... they could have been from the van or from mud in the canal.'

'I know. I know. Anything else?'

He raised up the length of rough white timber that had not been planed. It was about 4" long x 4" wide x 1" thick. 'This is the piece of wood that was used to jam the accelerator. It appears to have been part of a packing crate of some sort. It has part of a word stencilled on it. Three letters only, "ønd". I think it might be part of a company or an address. The whole word might have been stencilled across a crate, this piece catching only the three letters.'

Angel nodded. 'I know what you mean, Don.'

'According to my researches, that strange looking "ø" is represented like that in Norway.'

Angel's eyes narrowed. 'Norway?' Angel said.

'I don't know where it fits in the puzzle, sir. Indeed, it may not have any significance at all, just a piece of timber that was handy for the murderer the time he was planning to dump the van in the canal.'

'Thanks Don. Frankly, I have not the remotest idea if it is significant or not. There are no links to Norway that I can think of in this case.'

Taylor smiled. 'It'll come to you in due course, sir.'

'You know, Don. I thought this job would get easier as I got older.'

'You'll get there, sir. You always do. They say, like the Mountie, you always get your man.'

'This case might be the exception to the rule, Don. I mean, what's the point of all these murders? I can't even find a solid reason...explanation. Where's the motive? We are not dealing with logic. We are not dealing with a human being who wants something tangible like a diamond, an estate, a billion pounds, a lover, a throne or a title. We are dealing with a lunatic, a phantom, a spectre, who wants to annihilate ordinary innocent people who played characters in a disastrous production of a play twenty years ago. But, why? And it's somebody very close, Don. Somebody who was in the production, who knows what went on then and, perhaps more worrying, somebody who knows what's happening now.'

'Well, is there anything more I can do, sir.'

'No, Don. Just keep on doing what you do best.'

Taylor smiled. 'Like you, sir.'

Angel wasn't smiling. 'We don't always get choices in this world.'

'No, sir,' Taylor said and he went out and closed the door.

Angel thought about the piece of wood, the letter strange letter "ø" and Norway for a few moments, then shrugged and reached out for the phone and tapped in a number. It was to the hospital mortuary. 'I want to speak to Dr Mac, please.'

'You want to know about Angus Peel, Michael?' Mac said. 'Well there's very little to say.'

'Anything unusual, Mac. I am not interested in his statistics.'

'He was stabbed, as you know. It *was* in the aorta. Same weapon, I would say. Died instantly. He was dead before he hit the water. Nothing you would describe as unusual in this case. What else do you want to know?'

Angel sighed. 'Tell me, Mac, in your experience, could a woman have committed all these murders?'

'Oh yes. Doesn't need much strength to stick a sharp instrument into a person's heart. It takes a bit of knowledge, and it might take a bit of muscle to hold them still while you do it.'

'That's what I thought. Thanks, Mac.' Angel replaced the phone.

He blew out a long sigh, then leaned back in the chair and began to massage his chin. There were no breaks in the case anywhere. Everywhere was proving to be a dead end. And there were two obstacles that seemed insurmountable: the two loose hairs on the back of Luke Redman's hand. They *must* have belonged to the murderer. And the lab report said they belonged to a woman, and a woman with East Asian ancestry. There was only one woman, Margaret Ireland, in the case and, although she had no alibi for the times of all three murders, she was as English as he was. East Asian meant that one of the murderer's forbears, at least one, came from the Far East. That's literally from the Persian Gulf to Wallace's Line. That takes in India, Japan, China and then as far as the East Indies. There was no woman in the case, as far as he knew, with those qualifications. It required some thinking about. There was another possibility. Unlikely, but possible. That the hairs had been deliberately planted by the murderer. It would show an understanding of forensic procedure. However, if they had been planted, why weren't there similar plants on the other victim's? Well, on Ingrid Underwood's body anyway. You would have expected *that*. Angel pondered on that a while then returned to believing firmly that the hairs had *not* been planted by the murderer. They were there by chance. They must have been from the murderer. He knew it didn't make sense but he had wrestled with conundrums like this before. There would be an explanation. It just took time.

Supposing Lamb or Franks was a woman. That would explain it. He thought about it a few moments. He tried to imagine them in wigs and dresses. It was ridiculous. There was nothing effeminate about either of them. Then he remembered the old adage. If it walks like a duck, and squawks like a duck, it's a duck.

An unhappy thought crossed his mind. He remembered that Margaret Ireland would have to be released tomorrow. He couldn't hold her any longer. If she was innocent, she'd be unprotected against Lamb and Franks, and Angel was helpless to protect her.

There were times when this job was impossible and this was one of those times. All this science around but none to help him in this case. He was thinking that the murderer deposited Peel's body in the canal to frustrate SOCO by contaminating any forensic that might have been on his clothes. If so, why wasn't the murderer worried when he murdered Ingrid Underwood? Sitting so close to her like that he would almost certainly have left a speck, a hair, something. He was wearing a sheet, sandals and a wig.

Then something hit him like a thunderbolt. A wig! Some women sold their hair for money, particularly Indian women. Witnesses had said that the murderer seen running up and down in early Roman clothes was wearing a wig. The two loose hairs found on the back of Luke Redman's hand could have been from the wig the murderer was wearing, which was made from the hair of a woman who was from the orient. That was it! There was the explanation. The DNA result showed genes compatible with a female from the orient. Why didn't he think of it before? The murderer must still be Kenneth Lamb, Tom Franks or Margaret Ireland. And Lamb and Franks were still at large. Indeed Angel had encouraged the two men to go into hiding. What a farce! Angel closed his eyes. It would be funny if it wasn't so terrifyingly dangerous. However, he had no actual evidence that any of the last three survivors from the *Nero* production *was* the murderer, and he had pressed his investigations on them as far as Judge's Rules allowed. And that meant that now he had no more lines of inquiry. That was it.

He would have to consider other avenues of investigation. He would create new lines of inquiry, because doing something was better than doing nothing! He would go back to the heart of the case.

He reached out for the phone.

'Is that *The Bromersley Chronicle*? Can I speak to Mr Jack Hanger, please? This is Detective Inspector Angel, Bromersley police.'

'Good morning, Inspector. What can I do for you? How are you getting along with that serial murder case?'

'Ah, Mr Hanger. It's difficult, I must confess. I am looking for some more information. You may remember the man who was severely burned in that theatre production was called Malcolm Malloy.'

'Yes, I remember.'

'Can you tell me what happened to him? I know that he died. I expect your paper reported his death.'

'Just let me load it up. What was the date of that fire again? Do you remember?'

'Almost exactly twenty years ago, May 1989. He died shortly afterwards, probably in June.'

'Won't take much finding. What do you want to know exactly?'

'All you've got, if you don't mind.'

'Pleased to be of help, Inspector.'

There was a short pause then Hanger said, 'It's coming. It's very slow this morning...here it is. Yes, inspector. It's a two-inch double-column report on page one bottom right-hand corner.'

'Would you read it out to me, please?'

'Certainly,' Hanger said. 'The headline is, "Bromersley actor dies of burns aged 25". Then it goes on, "Malcolm Malloy, the promising young actor, died on Monday night. He was severely burned on stage while playing the eponymous *Nero* on the opening night at the Variety Theatre last April. He had been taken by ambulance to Bromersley General, where he was examined and treated for 80% burns. Later he was transferred to the specialist burns unit at Skiptonthorpe Cottage Hospital where he died. The funeral is at St Edward's Parish Church at 2 p.m. on Friday next, 10 June. Funeral Directors, Jobson Hargreaves." And that's all, Inspector.'

'Thank you very much, Mr Hanger. Would you be kind enough to print off the piece for me and I'll arrange for it to be collected?'

'Of course. Goodbye.'

Angel then put a call through to the office of the Registrar of Births, Deaths and Marriages at Bromersley Town Hall.

'Detective Inspector Angel of Bromersley police. I am looking into the death of a Malcolm Malloy who died on 24 May 1989. Would you please tell me who reported the death?'

The information eventually came: 'The person who reported the death was a Mr Jonathan Parker-Snell.'

'Thank you,' he said and replaced the phone. He vaguely remembered the name. Jonathan Parker-Snell was the man who produced the play twenty years earlier and that he was one of the nineteen who had already died. He was surprised that the report of Malloy's death to the Registrar had not been made by a family member. He pulled open a desk drawer and took out the local telephone book. With a name like Parker-Snell, he shouldn't have any difficulty finding a surviving relative, if he had one. There was only one entry and it was a W. Parker-Snell. He dialled the number. After being put through to a telephonist and a secretary, Angel managed to be able to speak to the man. He thought he must be a busy man.

'I am making inquiries about the late Jonathan Parker-Snell, sir,' Angel said.

'That was my uncle, Inspector. He died about ten years ago. How can I help?'

'Was he interested in the theatre and the production of plays?'

'Indeed he was. He had been a professional actor in his younger years, then latterly he coached and produced local amateur plays and light opera. Why?'

'I am looking into the history of a Malcolm Malloy, a young actor who was directed by your uncle in a play, and who died following an accidental fire in 1989. Can you help me?'

'That was a bit before my time, Inspector, but I remember my uncle told my late father and me something about him.'

'It was your uncle who reported his death to the Registrar of Births, Deaths and Marriages. It's usually a job for the next of kin.'

'I don't think there was any family, Inspector. And I don't believe Mr Malloy left anything much of value, either. I remember my uncle cleared out his flat, settled his bills and paid for the funeral.'

'Do you happen to know where Mr Malloy lived?'

'He had a flat on Huddersfield Road, I believe. I don't know which one.'

'Thank you very much, sir.'

He cancelled the call and rang the undertakers, Jobson Hargreaves. He was soon speaking to Mr Hargreaves Senior. 'I'm making inquiries about the funeral of a Malcolm Malloy who died on 24 May and whose funeral was on the 10 June 1989.'

'That's almost twenty years ago, Inspector. It will take me a few minutes to find the right order book.'

He eventually came back and said, 'I took the order, Inspector. It's in my writing. Mr Malcolm Malloy. Now what did you want to know?'

'What was Mr Malloy's address?'

'It's given here as Skiptonthorpe Cottage Hospital. That's where we would have had to collect his remains.'

Angel rubbed his chin. The place was ten miles out, towards the moors. It had been closed down years. Who gave you the order?'

'A Mr J. Parker-Snell.'

'And who signed the death certificate?'

'It's just a squiggle of course, but thankfully, it's typed underneath. Dr Cambridge.'

'And was Mr Malloy buried or cremated?'

'Buried. Strange, I remember. He's in a quiet plot by the wall in Bromersley Central Cemetery. Plot 1505.'

Angel blinked. He was very surprised. He fully expected to be told he had been cremated. 'Thank you very much, Mr Hargreaves.'

He replaced the phone, went out of the office, and dashed down the corridor, past the cells to the back door. He jumped into the BMW and drove through the town centre and out on the Sheffield Road to the first traffic lights. He turned left and left again and he was on Cemetery Road. He passed a procession of shiny limousines, which had just left the cemetery. A man was closing the wrought-iron gates.

Angel parked up the car, got out and went over to him.

'Are you the cemetery manager?'

'I'm the gravedigger, sir,' the man said with a smile. 'But I accept the promotion willingly.'

Angel's tact had worked. 'It's all done with machinery now, isn't it?' he said nodding towards a small diesel-driven digger on tracks.

'Aye. You've sussed me out. What can I do for you?'

'I'm looking for grave number 1505, a Mr Malcolm Malloy.'

'1505? That'll be on the south side, by the wall. Come on. I'll walk you down.'

'Thank you.'

The two men trudged silently down the long path, the gravedigger leading. When almost at the end, the gravedigger took a stride off the flagstone on to grass, around some headstones and then up to the cemetery boundary wall. Angel followed. The gravedigger stopped, pointed at an unmarked plot and said, 'That's it. 1505.'

Angel looked down at the grassed-over plot with no headstone or grave edging and frowned. 'Are you sure?' he said.

The gravedigger was adamant. He fished around over the plot in the dandelions with his fingers and found a grey aluminium marker with the number 1505 embossed on it stuck into the earth. He pointed it out to Angel.

Angel acknowledged that it was 1505, nodded, thanked him, returned to his car and drove straight to Bromersley General Hospital. After a good deal of persuasive talking to the hospital secretary, the young man said he would need to consult his several masters. Angel hung around waiting in the secretary's office until sanctions were granted. Then he was shown to a small general office behind the lifts, where he was invited to wait. Twenty minutes later, a porter wheeled in a trolley of dusty files from the cellar for Angel's perusal.

'There you are, sir. That's everything there is on Skiptonthorpe Cottage Hospital from 1 January 1989 until it closed in May. You can leave them here when you've done. But please don't muck them up.'

'I won't,' Angel said. 'And thank you.'

Angel dived into the files and soon found out that Malloy was admitted to the hospital at 9.42 p.m. on 11 April 1989. There were details of the doctor who examined him, treated him, prescribed the trauma routine for him, and many details of his welfare and his physical reaction to it. He was diagnosed as having 80 per cent burns. Angel found out that the morning following the night he was admitted, Malloy was transferred to the cottage hospital, Skiptonthorpe, for specialist burns treatment. The treatment seemed to be almost exclusively trauma nursing. He noted that he had been written up for a visit from a psychiatrist and several visits from a prosthesis clinic technician. As much as Angel could interpret medical terminology, Malloy seemed at that time to have been dangerously ill.

After two hours of wading through results of endless tests, unintelligible notes and daily reports, Angel looked up wearily and rubbed his eyes. He wondered whether all this was leading him any nearer to catching the murderer. On the last page of Malloy's notes was a printed floor plan of the ward indicating the door, sink, the placing of the furniture, and so on. Angel noticed that there were only two beds shown, and across each bed in blue Biro was written a patient's name. His heart leaped when he saw the name of the one who shared the ward with Malloy.

He sat back in the chair and looked round the empty overheated office, stunned, as if someone had hit him with Strangeways's tower. He dived back into the files and spent another hour searching, reading and making notes.

Then he tidied all the papers in the files, returned them in their proper order to the trolley and came out of the little office. He went out to his car. He made a call at the electoral roll office at the Town Hall then he drove straight to Dr Suliman to get a warrant. Angel almost always approached Dr Suliman because he was usually the most accessible JP in Bromersley, and warrants were almost always needed at short notice.

By the time Angel reached the station, it was five minutes past five. He looked in the CID office but it was empty. He ran into his office and reached for the phone. Nobody was answering the phone in the SOCO's office either.

He heard the distant clang of a metal locker door followed by the closing of a door up the corridor. He slammed down the phone and rushed out of the office, hoping to see one of his team.

It was DS Carter.

He pursed his lips and rubbed his chin. She was one of his team, of course. But for the job he had to do, he reckoned it needed a man.

She walked up to him like a young gazelle.

'Good night, sir,' she said with a nervous smile.

She passed him.

He didn't reply. He couldn't. He watched her. He was thinking. He had a warrant to arrest a serial killer in his pocket. He'd like to keep it 'in the family'. Should he get uniform to assist him now? Or ask her? Or leave it until the morning?'

'Sergeant Carter,' he called.

She stopped in the corridor and turned. 'I thought you were going to ignore me, sir?'

'No. No,' he said, rubbing his chin. 'Lot on my mind.' He ran the tip of his tongue along his bottom lip. 'Are you in a hurry?'

She blinked. 'No, sir,' she said as she walked back towards him.

'Like to earn a bit of overtime? I am hopefully going out to arrest the serial killer.'

Her eyes and mouth opened wide. 'Sir!' she said.

He frowned. 'I take it that's a yes. Bring some handcuffs.'

CHAPTER FIFTEEN

Angel stopped the car outside 12a Mulberry Place, a big old Victorian house and pulled on the handbrake. 'I don't know whether he'll be at home or not. I'll try him on the front door. You go round the back. And be careful.'

Carter dashed off.

Angel walked slowly up the steps to give time for Carter to get in position. He looked at the unwashed windows and the dirty step. He frowned when he observed that the curtains in both of the front rooms were closed. He noticed the cobweb across the corner of the front door as he banged the knocker hard and loud. There was no reply. He waited a few moments then repeated the battering. There was still no reply. He went round the side of the house and saw Carter waiting by the back door.

She saw him and came over.

'No reply,' he said, licking his lower lip with the tip of his tongue.

'What now, sir.'

'We're going to break in.'

She looked round for a window to break.

Angel noticed what she was doing. 'No,' he said.

He walked across to the back door and peered at the lock. 'It's only a two lever,' he said. 'Shouldn't take long.'

Carter watched in surprise as he took a slim case of lock-picking tools out of his inside pocket. 'Hold this for me,' he said.

She held the open case for him.

Firstly, he sorted out a blank key about the size of the lock, covered one side with white chalk, inserted it in the lock, turned it anticlockwise as far as it would go, withdrew it and checked it for marks. It told him what he needed to know. Then he carefully introduced a pick into the keyhole and then another. He soon had the first lever and had to fish round for the second. It took him a minute or so. He thought he had found it. He applied some pressure. There was a click and it was done. He returned the picks, the blank key and chalk to the case, took it from her, closed it and dropped it back into his inside pocket.

Carter said, 'Is it unlocked?'

He nodded, turned the knob and pushed open the door.

'Anybody here?' he called. 'This is the police.'

The door led straight into a large, old fashioned kitchen, meanly furnished and in need of a good clean.

'Anybody here? This is the police,' they called several times.

They walked quickly through it into a hall. It wasn't a pleasant sight. A corner of the hall had the wallpaper peeling off. Cobwebs were draped from corner to corner. The floor was uncarpeted. There was the smell of stale food. There was no furniture.

Four doors led out of the hall.

Angel indicated to Carter to look in the rooms.

He looked in the nearest room, which was uncarpeted and had no furniture in it. A second was also empty. A third room was in darkness, the curtain was drawn to. He switched on the light. It had a computer on a bench, a large-screen TV, a chair and piles of magazines and newspapers on the floor.

He put his hand on the top of the TV screen expecting it to be cold. It wasn't.

He sucked in air. A thumping started in his chest. He realized the murderer could not be far away. He suddenly thought about Carter. He dashed out into the hall. She was on the stairs. He was relieved that she was all right. She saw him. Her face brightened. He ran up behind her.

'Weird, sir?' she said.

'He's in the house,' he whispered. 'Be careful.'

She gasped then gawped back at him, with big, startled eyes.

'How do you know?' she said.

He didn't reply. He wished he had brought somebody with muscles like Gawber. He overtook her and reached the top of the stairs. He looked in one room. It was also unfurnished.

Carter looked in the room opposite.

He came back on the landing and had gone into another room when he heard her gasp.

'Sir! Sir!' Carter yelled.

'Yes. Have you found him?'

He dashed out to the landing and bumped into her.

Her hands were shaking in front of her. She saw them as if they weren't hers. Her face tightened. She stopped shaking and put them down by her side as if she was purposely steeling herself.

'Have you found him?' Angel said.

'No, sir.'

'What is it, then?' he said.

Her eyes tracked to the door of the room she had just come out of. 'In there, sir.'

Angel went up to the open door. His nose twitched. There was an unusual smell. He became immediately aware of warm air round his cheeks, ears and hands, and a smell of hot wax. As he went inside, he saw the amazing sight of many candles and nightlights lit - some on a table, some on the floor, and at the far side of the room, some on a dressing table reflected in a mirror. Then Angel saw that draped on a wall were four white bed sheets heavily stained in blood. He reckoned they would be the sheets worn as Roman-type garments by the murderer when he killed Luke Redman, Ingrid Underwood and Angus Peel.

He breathed in and out deeply. His pulse rate was very fast.

It was a big room. Probably the master bedroom. The candles produced an oppressive heat and a camphor like smell.

Carter came up close to him and said. 'Where is he, sir?' Angel shook his head. 'Don't know.'

He was wondering where he was, also thinking that possession of those sheets alone with his DNA as well as the victim's on them would be enough to convict him and put him away forever.

There was a high table in front of the sheets, with four photographs, in frames, of the characters in Roman dress from the production twenty years earlier, and four brass candlesticks on it, each holding huge candles decorated with glitter and what looked like brightly coloured glass stones in red, green, blue and amber.

'It's a shrine,' Angel said.

Carter's jaw dropped open. 'A shrine?'

They ventured further into the large room and saw another table with a lamp on it, also a large mirror and hat blocks on it. There was a golden-brown man's wig on one, and a wreath of laurel leaves on the other. To the left of the mirror was a steel box with twenty or more sticks and pots of stage make-up, and to the right, a big open pot of cold cream, and three open packets of crepe hair in different colours.

They were so absorbed in all these materials that they failed to notice a man silently appear from behind one of the bloody bedsheets. He had his hands in his pockets.

He stared at them for a moment then said, 'Ah. Inspector Angel and a beautiful young lady.'

His voice was as cold as the Christmas icicles that hang from Strangeways' roof. 'Breaking and entering my humble home. What are you doing here?'

Startled, they turned to face him.

Angel was on his mettle. 'We've come to arrest you,' he said.

'Ha. You'll never arrest me.'

'It's Mr Lamb,' Carter said.

'Oh you know me, Miss. I'm flattered,' he said.

'It's not Kenneth Lamb,' Angel said. 'It's Malcolm Malloy, in a mask.'

Carter frowned.

The man sniggered. 'You're right, as always, dear Inspector. Your reputation remains unsullied. You will be able to go to your grave knowing that you were right again. However did you find out? I thought I had covered my tracks perfectly.'

'The hospital records, Malloy. You should have destroyed them.'

'The hospital records? Huh. I didn't need to. The switch was perfect. The man in the next bed died of similar burns to mine. It was an easy matter to wheel the beds round, swap over the notes, put an extra roll of bandage over the dead man's face, and the switch was made. The hospital was closing down the following day. The staff were in chaos. They were leaving for other jobs. I pretended to be asleep when the idiot nurse looked at me, then let the undertaker come in and take the dead man out. The plan was perfect.'

'Wonderful,' Angel said ironically.

'Yes. I thought so,' Malloy said. 'You didn't say what I missed.'

'You didn't destroy the ward plan. I only had to see the name of the other man in the ward, and it showed up the whole nasty business.'

'Damn. I should have been more thorough. Damn. Damn. Damn.'

'You probably ruined his family's life, Malloy.'

'Huh. He didn't have any family, Inspector. Like me. He didn't have anybody close. He didn't have any visitors. Don't you think I hadn't thought of that? I watched that *very carefully*. We shared the ward for almost six weeks, we became very close. He had to have face reconstruction, as I had. It made us both look like freaks. *Freaks*! I have had to wear a prosthetic chin and half cheek ever since. But my instruction in make-up at stage school came in very handy. You never noticed, did you? If you didn't have to touch my face, you would never have known.'

'Of course I knew. I knew it wasn't Lamb who stole the sheets. Like I knew you weren't Lamb when you appeared so dramatically just now.'

'How could you know? How did you know? My height is the same as his. The suit is similar to the one he wears. The mask is a fair likeness, and the skin colour identical!'

'You have blue eyes, he has brown, and the mask does not flex and tighten naturally when you speak.'

Malloy breathed in noisily. He was not pleased. 'There are *limits* to what one can expect of a mask, Inspector.'

'What did you start it all for?' Angel said. 'Why murder the people who were your friends.'

'They were not my friends. They were my competitors. While I was three years in and out of hospital, in unspeakable pain and being carved about, they were making relationships, marrying, having children, running businesses, establishing practices, becoming famous. Doing all the things normal people do. But not I. All I could do was take a backroom job, a humble clerk, where hardly anybody saw me. With a face like mine, I couldn't even get a job as the hunchback of Notre Dame, much less as a leading man. I couldn't kiss a woman – on stage or off – for fear she would be repelled by the coldness of my plastic lip. Why should it happen to me? What had I done? Why couldn't it have happened to someone else? There are plenty of stupid, worthless, motiveless people out there in the world. Why me? I was set for great things. I was greatly talented. I was ready for all the Shakespearean, Dickensian and every other part. There isn't a character I could not have played magnificently. I was set to pick up all the awards. Everybody said so. By now, I would have had a cupboard full of Oscars. My name would have been linked with all the big Hollywood names. I would have been chancellor of universities. Awarded the CBE. I would have been worth millions. Women would have been clamouring for my attention and I would have been swatting them away like flies. I would have made love to every desirable woman in the world and been searching for more. There would have been no end to it. Alas, it was not to be.'

Angel sniffed. 'No, it was not.' He stepped forward and said, 'Malcolm Malloy, I am arresting you on -'

Malloy suddenly pulled his right hand, holding the silver dagger, out of his pocket. He held it up high. 'Stay where you are, Inspector. Nobody is arresting anybody.'

Angel froze. His heart pounded.

Carter stared up at the weapon.

Angel took a deep breath, turned back to Malloy and said, 'I have started the notice of arrest, I *have* to finish it.'

'I have not finished my mission, Inspector. There are still two members of the conspiracy that have to be disposed of.'

'No, Malloy. Put down the dagger down. Your killing spree is finished.'

Carter suddenly said, 'Come on, Mr Malloy. I think your description of the mad man who has been badly treated has been most wonderfully portrayed and if it had been part of a screen trial, I reckon you would most certainly have got the part.'

Angel glanced at her, his mouth open. He wondered if she had gone mad.

'Really?' Malloy said. 'Do you think so? You are so much more understanding than the Inspector.'

Angel blinked.

'But I do think you should put the dagger down,' Carter said. 'You have made your point most eloquently, I thought. You know, Mr Malloy, it might be possible for you to take up writing plays for the stage or television. You could become another George Bernard Shaw or Alan Ayckbourn. Had you never thought of it?'

Malloy's voice changed. It was softer and thoughtful. 'Writing plays?'

'If you have to go away for a while, you could write a play or a whole series for television. You would only need paper and a pen.'

Malloy's voice changed. 'I've certainly lots of ideas. Characters are always bouncing around in my head at night; they keep me awake. I never sleep for long. Some nights I never sleep at all.'

Angel watched and listened. He didn't move.

'You need some peace and quiet, Mr Malloy,' she said. 'Let's start by getting rid of that dagger.'

Malloy blinked. Thought a moment, then lowered his hand with the dagger in it to his side.

'Shall I take it, Malcolm? Can I call you Malcolm?'

'Nobody has called me Malcolm in years. What's your name?'

She stepped up to him with her hand open.

She forced a smile at Malloy. 'DS Carter,' she said.

Malloy looked at the dagger, gave a little shrug, turned the dagger round so that he was holding the blade and offered it to her.

Malloy was about three feet away from them both.

She reached out for it.

Angel held his breath.

Malloy smiled, then when she was almost touching the handle, he swiftly pulled his hand back and said, 'Do you think I'm so stupid?' In a split second he reversed his grip so that he was holding the dagger firmly by the handle and he reached up to make a stab at her.

Angel, who had not taken his eyes off the dagger, dashed forward and made a snatch for his wrist. Malloy looked amazed. He pulled against Angel's grip but it was useless. He withdrew his hand from the other pocket and Carter saw that he had another knife. Malloy pressed the end and a blade flicked out, which he plunged into Angel's back.

Carter saw blood spurt out, screamed, looked round for a weapon of some sort. She reached up to the crude altar beside her, snatched up the nearest candlestick, tossed out the lighted candle and landed a tremendous series of blows at Malloy's head, chest and hand until her strength ran out.

Eventually, Malloy dropped the flick knife, turned, stared into her eyes and fell full length in front of her.

Angel fell over the top of him, now holding the dagger in his hand.

Flames flared up around the altar from the discarded candle.

'Cuff him,' Angel said panting and got to his feet.

As she did so, on her knees, she said, 'I may have killed him.'

Angel saw the flick knife and kicked it towards the door. 'Self-defence, if you have.'

'Yes, but -'

'He might be better off. If he's alive, he'll be sent to Rampton and never see the light of day again.'

Suddenly there was a roar of yellow flames as one of the sheets behind the altar caught fire. There was a carpet on fire and the covering on the altar was alight. The whole room was ablaze with candles and with fabrics and curtains on fire.

They set about stamping out the burning fabrics, dragging them to the floor and stamping on them. Smoke added to the confusion. There was a shortage of oxygen causing them to gasp. The flames took hold on the wallpaper and the curtains round the window. Angel took off his coat and tried to damp down the flames. As fast as they put one fire out, another developed.

Angel took out his mobile and tapped in a number.

'Control Room.'

'This is DI Angel. Send an ambulance to 12a Mulberrry Place. Also report a fire there, also send two uniformed men ASAP. Don't mess about. Matter of life and death.'

'Right, sir.'

He closed the phone.

The figure on the floor wriggled.

Angel noticed and looked at Carter. She'd seen it too.

More flames roared up behind them.

'Let's get him out.'

Malloy was on his face, his handcuffed hands behind his back. They each put an arm through his and tried to move him. It was slow but they dragged him on to the landing, which was filling with smoke. One of Malloy's trouser bottoms had caught fire. Angel stamped on it and put it out.

The room was an inferno of flames and candles and the heat was increasing. Angel, shielding his face with his arm, went back to the door and tried to close it. It was too late it fell to pieces in flames.

Malloy moved again. His eyes opened. Carter stooped down to look at him.

Angel looked back into the room. 'We can't do any more in there,' he said. He moved further away from the doorway and began to put on his coat. There was blood on it. He looked at it surprised. Carter saw him.

'He caught you with the knife.'

'Where? I didn't know.'

Angel found that it was near his side. It didn't hurt, but it was oozing blood.

Carter looked at his bloody shirt and pulled a face.

There was a crash as something in the room fell down. The fire had developed a roar, and a regular crackling of burning timber.

Malloy groaned.

They looked down at him. His mask had partly melted in the heat and the scuffle.

Angel said, 'We'll have to get out of here.'

'How,' she said.

He looked down at the floor said, 'Hey, Malloy. Can you stand up?'

'What?'

'Can you stand up?'

Malloy slowly shuffled round into a sitting position, then Angel pulled him up by the back of his shirt neck.

'Are you all right?'

The man blinked and swayed a couple of times.

Angel said, 'Can you walk?'

Malloy struggled with his shoulders and arms. 'My hands. What have you done to my hands?'

'Are you all right?' Angel called out above the roar of the fire.

'You bastards. You're a right pair of bastards.'

'Can you hear me, Malloy?'

'Of course I can bloody well hear you.'

Angel looked at Carter and said, 'You do it, lass.'

She nodded, turned back to the man and said, 'Malcolm Malloy, I am arresting you for the murder of Luke Redman, Ingrid Underwood and Angus Peel. You do not have to say anything...'

CHAPTER SIXTEEN

It was 8.28 a.m. the following morning, Thursday, 4 June. Angel arrived at his office whistling, 'Oh what a beautiful morning. Oh what a beautiful day...'

He hadn't reached his chair before the phone rang. It was Taylor. He sounded very bright. 'I hear you got him, sir? Congratulations. Who would have thought it was Malloy all the time.'

'Thank you, Don. You did your share.'

'By the way, sir, this morning I realized that that piece of timber with the fancy Norwegian letter "ø" stencilled on it, used by him to sprag the accelerator pedal in the van, would likely have been from a crate of newsprint used by the printing press of *The Bromersley Chronicle*.'

'Most likely,' Angel said. 'We'll make a detective out of you yet, Don.'

Taylor grinned.

Angel replaced the phone.

There was a knock on the door.

'Come in,' he said.

It was Ahmed with the morning's post. 'Good morning, sir. And congratulations. I understand you've solved the serial murder case. And that you've arrested that clerk from

The Bromersley Chronicle office. That's great, sir. We all knew you would do it.'

Angel pursed his lips, then said, 'Well, DS Carter needs credit for making the actual arrest.'

He looked surprised. 'Really? And she only weighs eight stone, four pounds.'

Angel frowned. 'How the blazes do you know what she weighs?'

'We were talking about diets and stuff, and she told me, sir,' Ahmed said putting the envelopes on the desk in front of him.

Angel frowned and shook his head. 'The things you talk about...'

Ahmed went out.

Angel began fingering through the envelopes, when there was another knock.

'Come in.'

It was Carter. She came in all smiles, carrying a notepad. 'Good morning, sir. I hope you slept well.'

He looked up, pointed to the chair by his desk.

She sat down.

Angel said, 'You don't have to continue the social chit-chat you used to mesmerize Malcolm Malloy last night, you know.'

'It worked, sir,' she said with a big smile.

'Not really. Anyway, it might work on vain people. Not on hard nuts like me.'

She laughed then said, 'How's your back, sir? What did they say at the hospital?'

'It's all right. In their lingo, it didn't perforate any vital organs.'

She nodded. 'I bet it's painful.'

He frowned and looked at her. 'What do you want anyway?' he said.

'A question, sir.'

'Go on.'

'I only remembered this morning. In that room...that shrine. There were *four* bloodstained sheets hanging down.

And *four* photographs on the table. Yet, as far as we know, there are only three victims?'

'Yes,' he replied and licked his bottom lip with the tip of his tongue. 'I noticed.'

'Did you manage to see who the people were in the photographs?'

'No, I didn't. I had a few...other things on my mind.'

'Yes, sir. Of course.'

The phone rang. He reached out for it. 'Angel.'

The caller said something to which Angel said, 'Right, sir. I'll deal with it straightaway.'

He replaced the phone and turned to Carter. 'That was the Super. A triple nine just in. Another body with a wound in the chest. The landlord of the Wentworth Arms has found the body of a man behind some dustbins at the back of the pub.'

'*That's* the fourth victim, sir.'

Angel nodded. He rubbed his chin, sighed and said, 'It'll be Kenneth Lamb. He lives at...lived at 72 Wentworth View. It's just behind there.'

'Must have happened sometime yesterday,' Carter said. 'He *wouldn't* go into hiding.'

Angel's lips tightened back against his teeth. He shook his head. 'It would have saved his life. Why don't people listen to us?'

'Poor Mr Lamb,' Carter said, then looked down and shook her head.

Angel stood up and said, 'Well, come on, Flora. Let's get on with it.'

She looked at him in surprise.

THE END

OTHER BOOKS BY ROGER SILVERWOOD

YORKSHIRE MURDER MYSTERIES
Book 1: THE MISSING NURSE
Book 2: THE MISSING WIFE
Book 3: THE MAN IN THE PINK SUIT
Book 4: THE MORALS OF A MURDERER
Book 5: THE AUCTION MURDERS
Book 6: THE MISSING KILLER
Book 7: THE UMBRELLA MURDERS
Book 8: THE MISSING MILLIONAIRE
Book 9: THE MISSING THIEF
Book 10: FIND THE LADY
Book 11: THE MISSING MODEL
Book 12: MURDER IN BARE FEET
Book 13: THE MISSING HUSBAND
Book 14: THE CUCKOO CLOCK MURDERS
Book 15: SHRINE TO MURDER

FREE KINDLE BOOKS AND OFFERS

Please join our mailing list for free Kindle crime thriller, detective, mystery, and romance books and new releases, as well as news on Roger's next book!
www.joffebooks.com/contact/

Thank you for reading this book. If you enjoyed it please leave feedback on Amazon, and if there is anything we missed or you have a question about then please get in touch. The author and publishing team appreciate your feedback and time reading this book.

www.joffebooks.com

Follow us on Facebook, Instagram and Twitter
@joffebooks

We hate typos too but sometimes they slip through.
Please send any errors you find to
corrections@joffebooks.com
We'll get them fixed ASAP. We're very grateful to eagle-eyed readers who take the time to contact us.

Printed in Great Britain
by Amazon

60479069R00109